CAMDEN COUNTY LIBRARY
203 LAUREL ROAD
VOORHEES, NJ 08043

0 01 01 0366761 3

No Place
for a Lady

LARGE TYPE F Smi   APR 0 2 1997

Smith, Joan, 1938-

No place for a lady /

1997

D0555038

APR - 1 1997

DEMCO

CAMDEN COUNTY LIBRARY
203 LAUREL ROAD
VOORHEES, NJ 08043

Joan Smith

No Place for a Lady

WHEELER
PUBLISHING, INC.
ROCKLAND, MA

★ AN AMERICAN COMPANY ★

Copyright © 1994 by Joan Smith

All rights reserved.

Published in Large Print by arrangement with
Ballantine Books, a division of Random House, Inc.
in the United States and Canada.

Wheeler Large Print Book Series.

Set in 16 pt. Plantin.

Library of Congress Cataloging-in-Publication Data

Smith, Joan, 1938-
    No place for a lady / Joan Smith.
        p. (large print) cm.(Wheeler large print book series)
    ISBN 1-56895-424-7 (softcover)
    1. Large type books. I. Title. II. Series
[PR9199.3.S5515N6 1997]
813'.54—dc21
                                                    97-3573
                                                        CIP

No Place
for a Lady

Chapter One

"There must be some mistake!" I said to Miss Thackery, as the carriage progressed from the polite precincts of Piccadilly into that infamous territory of tumbledown shacks called Long Acre. Yet I dared not pull the draw cord for John Groom to stop. Twilight was falling, and groups of ruffians loitered on the street corners, casting larcenous eyes at our rig.

"It is not exactly what I pictured, to be sure," Miss Thackery replied, with a bemused glance out the window.

As we swept past the corner, a shot rang out, and two or three of the loiterers took to their heels. John Groom did not have to be told to spring the horses. For the next ten minutes, we were batted back and forth in the carriage like a pair of shuttlecocks. Even Miss Thackery was shaken out of her customary placidity, and I was frightened out of my wits.

Papa had warned me of the horrors of London, but as he is a provincial clergyman who had not been to London himself for twenty years, I paid him scant heed. When Aunt Thalassa, my late mama's sister, left me a house in London, I had thought my troubles were over. Miss Thackery and I would either live in it, or if it was too grand for us, I would sell it and hire a set of rooms in some respectable district. Bath was another possibility.

Miss Thackery is like a mother to me. She is Papa's first cousin, who came to keep house for us when Mama died a dozen years ago. Life went along smoothly for a decade, then the Hennesseys moved into the parish. The family consisted of a managing widow and two pretty but vulgar daughters fifteen and sixteen years old. Within a month, Mrs. Hennessey had set her sights on Papa, and within a year she had half convinced him he was in love with her. She wears a sugary smile and is all sweetness when he is around, but the minute he leaves the room, the vinegar spurts forth. I have not been on this earth for one and twenty years without knowing a shrew when I see one.

I give Papa another two months of widowhood. The day she walks in the door as mistress of the rectory, I plan to walk out. I was so desperate I had even begun to consider marrying Sir Osbert Canning, who is forty and foolish. But then I had the letter from the solicitor telling me of the bequest from Aunt Thalassa, and I thought my problem was solved. Miss Thackery and I borrowed Papa's carriage and headed off to London to "dispose" of my inheritance. Papa's instructions were to evaluate it, sell the furnishings, and place the house with an estate agent for sale or rental, whichever was more profitable.

The solicitor had described the residence on Wild Street as "a large house in a semicommercial district." He did not specify exactly what sort of commerce went on there. I was beginning to suspect it was not only illegal but dangerous.

The carriage did not stop at Long Acre, however, but turned on to Drury Lane. The solicitor had mentioned Drury Lane as being near my aunt's house. Her late husband had been connected with the theater in an administrative capacity. Her occasional letters mentioned entertaining the very stars of the London stage: Kean, Siddons, Mrs. Jordan. I felt we must be approaching a fancy neighborhood.

I gazed with the keenest interest, marveling at the diversity of London. Odd that such motley homes were so close to my aunt's residence. Scattered amid tall, narrow, shabby buildings there were some houses of considerable elegance. Yet the people—a great many of them—entering and leaving these mansions did not look at all prosperous. A further confusion was caused by the flocks of ragged children playing on the street corners. Surely this was not how the wealthy lived, surrounded by poverty?

A closer look showed me that each "mansion," with its plate-glass-and-gilt cornices, bore a sign. Some proffered brandy, some cordials, but mostly they sold gin.

"They are gin palaces!" I exclaimed, and fell into a fit of giggles from sheer fatigue. We had been on the road since seven o'clock in the morning and had not eaten since noon.

"Mercy!" Miss Thackery said mildly, and peered out to see this interesting spectacle. "And the kiddies left in the streets with dark coming on, to look after themselves. They seem to be enjoying it, do they not? I daresay John Groom is lost. Your aunt was well to grass. You may be sure she did not live near here. Mullard has never been to London before, and despite the map Mrs. Hennessey provided him, I am sure we have passed that old stone church on the corner half a dozen times."

"I hope you are right," I said, and almost immediately the carriage turned the corner and drew to a stop.

"Lost, as I've said all along," Miss Thackery announced, not with satisfaction. She was not the sort who enjoyed seeing her doomful prognostications fulfilled. In fact, she was as nearly devoid of emotion as anyone I have ever met. The worst she has ever said of Mrs. Hennessey, for instance, is that "She certainly knows what she wants, and how to get it."

"Very likely Mullard is examining his map," I said.

The carriage lurched, and within two seconds, the groom's swarthy, haggard face appeared at the window. If anyone had had a worse day than Miss Thackery and myself, it was surely Mullard, who had never driven in any town larger than Bath. To us, living in Radstock, "the city" meant Bath. He flung open the carriage door and said, "This is it, Miss Irving."

"There must be some mistake!"

"Nay, this is Wild Street, second house from the corner of Kemble Street. I don't much care for the looks of it."

"Nor do I! This is not what I expected."

"Would you like me to take you to a hotel for the night? We could come back in the morning, after a good night's sleep."

It would take more than a night's sleep to get me over this disappointment. "You must be fagged, Mullard. Let us stay here for one night. If my aunt was living here, it must be…safe," I said, glancing around the disreputable spot. A group of urchins began to gather around our carriage.

Miss Thackery stared out into the gathering gloom and said in her matter-of-fact way, "You can always sell the house, Cathy. Any real estate in London is worth money."

We descended from the carriage with long faces—and took a good long look at my inheritance. To call the neighborhood shoddy was to flatter it, but at the least the commerce of gin palaces did not turn the corner on to Wild Street. The one tree on the block, a pretty spreading elm, was on my property. At the beginning of June, it was in full leaf. My house was not much different from the others on the block. This had been a residential area of some pretension to fashion fifty or so years ago. The houses were all tall, dark, gloomy edifices of smoke-laden brick, ranged close together with narrow laneways giving access to the rear. It would take an excellent fiddler to get the carriage through the narrow passage to the stable, which the solicitor had assured me was there. This was considered a great asset.

The house stood four stories high. On either side of the battered front door were two windows with some etched glass. The windows were repeated on the upper floors, minus the etching on the glass. The facade included a recessed veranda, which might have been enjoyable on a warm summer evening, except that it was tucked under the eaves of the attic. I was surprised to see so many of the windows showed lamps lit. Mrs. Scudpole, my late aunt's housekeeper, had been left in charge of the house. She would hear about this waste of candles!

Miss Thackery and I gathered our skirts up to avoid the dust on the walkway and went to tap at the front door. In place of a knocker there were some holes in the wood showing where one had been removed. We had the keys, but paid Mrs. Scudpole the courtesy of knocking, in case she wanted time to tidy her hair or change her apron. As we were soon to learn, such niceties never occurred to Mrs. Scudpole. The harridan who flung the door open looked as if she might have just darted off from one of the gin palaces. She did not actually reek of gin, but she was a slatternly woman with untidy hair and an apron that was a total stranger to soap and water.

"Ye'd be Mistress Irving then?" she said, looking from me to Miss Thackery.

"I am Miss Irving," I said, offering my hand, which she ignored. "And you, I collect, are Mrs. Scudpole?"

"Thass right, dearie. Come along inside. I'll make up some sangwidges for ye."

She led us into a dark hallway paneled in varnished wood, past a dusty staircase leading above, and thence into the saloon. Words seem inadequate to the chore of describing that saloon. It was large, dim, and lofty, and stuffed with every manner of mismatched furnishing and bibelot. Two or three carpets were on the floor, each smaller than the other and giving a glimpse of the one below. The top layer was deep blue, but we saw very little of it. There were not less than three mismatched sofas in the room—and a round dozen chairs. Against the walls, tables were piled on tables, with lamps wedged in wherever they could find room.

"Good gracious! Was Mrs. Cummings a dealer in used furniture?" I asked. I could not think of anything else to account for the jumble of lumber, and in the best room, too.

"I'll make the tea and sangwidges," was Mrs. Scudpole's reply. She left, and I looked at Miss Thackery. "What do you make of this?" I asked her.

She had walked forward to rub her hand over a small table that sat on a larger table near the grate. "I think this one is a Hepplewhite," she said. "The others will make good burning on a cold night."

There was a rattle at the window, and we both darted to see John Groom squeak the team of four and traveling carriage past the house. There was no sound of scraping or wood cracking, so I assumed he had executed the tight passage safely.

"I cannot imagine what my aunt was doing with all this...stuff," I said, looking helplessly about the room.

"Some ladies take strange notions in their older years," Miss Thackery said. My companion is forty-five, but she is one of those ladies who seems in a hurry to be old. She hides her pretty brown hair under a cap and wears gray gowns. Her face is long and thin, but not without some beauty. Her eyes are a pretty blue. When one can coax a smile out of her, she looks younger.

She continued, "Fortunately, with me it is only shawls and stockings I horde. I have nine shawls. I don't know why I keep buying them, except that I have the absurd idea I shall be cold in my old age."

"Not with all this lumber to burn," I said— in an effort to lighten the morose mood the room engendered.

7

"Whoever buys the house might take it furnished," she said. "You will be selling the house, now that you have seen it?" It was hardly even a question.

"Yes, certainly. I shall sell it, but I shan't stay with Papa if he marries *her*."

"She will be on your side in that, Cathy, have no fear. She will not want us underfoot. The rectory will hardly hold the Hennesseys and you and me besides. She has already mentioned that her girls would like your room, meaning that you and I can share mine."

"Good God! And he has not even proposed to her yet. What excuse did she give for looking at my bedroom?"

"She followed me upstairs the other day to help me carry down the hymnbooks I had been working on. She stopped at your door and walked right in."

"Encroaching creature!"

Mullard brought in our trunks. "Let me get my apron out before you take them to our rooms, Mullard," Miss Thackery said. "I cannot stand to sit in such filth. I can dust at least."

"It is nearly teatime. Let us wait," I suggested. Miss Thackery is a compulsive worker. She cannot tolerate dirt, and she dislikes to sit still.

"It may be awhile," Mullard said. "Mrs. Scudpole asked me to make the fire as soon as I delivered the trunks."

"Good gracious! She has let the fire go out. You might as well give me an apron, too, then," I said. "There is certainly plenty to be done here. We shan't waste time."

We removed our outer garments, put on the aprons, Mullard got us dust cloths, and we began dusting any surface that was accessible. It was not the way I had pictured beginning our little holiday in London. Before long, our hands and faces were liberally smudged, for the room was really shockingly dirty.

I turned at the sound of footfalls in the hallway. The tread was too hard and fast for Mrs. Scudpole. She moved at the speed of a tired tortoise. It could only be Mullard, but it was unlike him to come uninvited to the saloon— unless there was some trouble!

"He's lamed the horses in that narrow alley!" I exclaimed, and darted to the doorway.

I was nearly capsized by a young gentleman of the first stare. His hands reached out and gripped me by the upper arms to steady me. A pair of finely drawn eyebrows lifted high over a pair of intelligent gray eyes. His sleek head shone like the rich mahogany of a ripe chestnut. He wore it short, brushed forward in the stylish Brutus do. He was tall and well formed. On his broad shoulders sat an evening jacket of exquisite tailoring. A pristine white cravat, arranged in intricate folds, hinted at a streak of dandyism. He was so handsome he quite took my breath away.

"Who on earth are you, and what are you doing here?" I inquired. I had not meant to sound so abrupt, but surprise lent a sharp edge to my voice.

He gazed down at me with a quizzical smile on his face. "As you see, I am busy knocking young ladies off their feet. Are you all right?" I realized then that he was still holding on to me and drew back.

"I appear to be still in one piece," I replied.

"As to your other question, I am Mr. Alger." He bowed. "And you, of course, are Miss Irving."

"How did you know my name?" I asked in confusion.

"Why, I had it of Mrs. Scudpole. We have all been looking forward to meeting you, ma'am." His bold eyes traveled across my smudged face, down over my apron and grimy hands, apparently finding pleasure in the unsightly spectacle before him.

"You must excuse the way I look," I said, blushing furiously.

"But you look charming. Younger than I expected—and *much* prettier." His hand came out and flicked a bit of dust or cobweb from my cheek in a very familiar way. I shied away from him.

His eyes widened in astonishment, then he laughed. "If I did not know better, I would say you are frightened of me, Miss Irving."

"It is my house. Why should I be frightened of you?"

"That is precisely the question that occurred to me."

"You have not told me what you are doing here, Mr. Alger."

"I came to express my condolences on the death of your aunt."

"Thank you," I said. "I am sorry if I sounded abrupt. You took me by surprise. I did not see you come in the front door."

"I did not come in the door. Actually I was about to leave, but I wished to meet you, and—"

"If you did not come in via the door, may I ask how you did enter my house, sir?"

His eyebrows drew together in a frown. "What I meant to say was that I came down from upstairs."

"From upstairs? Did Mr. Duggan send you?"

Before he could reply, dragging footsteps announced the arrival of Mrs. Scudpole, bearing the tea tray. "G'd evening, Mr. Alger," she said, and brushed her way between us to deposit the tray on one of the many tables. "Cold mutton and cheese," she said grimly. "The butcher hasn't been paid in a month. If ye'll be wanting to eat here, you mun give me some blunt, Mistress."

Mr. Alger smiled in sympathy and said, "I shall leave you to your tea, ma'am. I look forward to meeting you again soon. And may I welcome you to Wild Street." He bowed and left. I don't believe I said a word in reply, or even curtsied.

"Who was that man?" I demanded of Mrs. Scudpole.

"Number 2A," was her unhelpful reply.

"I beg your pardon?"

"He's hired out suite 2A, hasn't he?"

"Where? What was he doing here?"

"Lives on the next floor, Mistress. I've nothing agin Mr. Alger. *He* always pays regular, unlike some."

"He *lives* here? Do you mean my aunt hired rooms?"

"Gorblimey, didn't you know? She's hired out every square inch above the first level, even the attics. Mind you, if it's only yourself and the old malkin," she said, tossing a glance at Miss Thackery, "there's plenty of room for you both on this floor." She leaned against a bow-fronted chest and settled in for a coze. "Now in your attics, you've got Professor Vivaldi. He's—"

"Thank you, Mrs. Scudpole. That will be all for now," I said, and stared at her until she stood up straight. "I shall speak to you after we have had tea. It has been a tiring day."

"You owe the butcher three pounds and fourpence," was her parting shot.

Meanwhile Miss Thackery had arranged the tea table. "I was watching from the doorway and wondered what that fine gentleman was doing upstairs," she said. "He looks well, but he would not be renting rooms in this part of town if he were respectable. I daresay he is an actor from Drury Lane."

"An actor! Yes, that would explain it. He was very handsome, was he not?"

"I thought his manner unpleasantly encroaching. You must give him a good setdown next time he comes mincing in."

She helped herself to a sandwich. "This mutton is quite good, Cathy," she said. "You will feel better able to cope with the situation after tea."

So saying, she poured tea into two chipped cups, and we had our first meal in our new home on Wild Street.

Chapter Two

After tea and cold mutton, we felt sufficiently restored to tour that part of the house my aunt Thal had occupied. Miss Thackery, who can find a reasonable explanation for anything, soon settled how my aunt came to be living in this squalid place and hiring out rooms.

"You recall, Cathy, her husband had something to do with the theater," she said. "A sort of manager, I believe. It would make sense for him to buy a house near Drury Lane. I daresay the neighborhood was respectable when he bought the house, and you know how difficult it is to move once you are established. So when her husband died, your aunt Thal just kept on here—and hired out rooms to pay the grocer. One can see how it came about."

"And all the unnecessary furnishings?" I asked, wondering how she would leap this hurdle without proclaiming my aunt a certifiable lunatic.

Mrs. Scudpole, who occasionally peeped her head in at us as we toured—and obviously had no notion of the meaning of the word "privacy"—spoke up from the doorway. "Only way she could get her blunt out of some of the folks she rented to, wasn't it? If they owed her, she seized their belongings. Bit by bit, she furnished the flats herself, but there was things left over, like."

"Quite a few things," I said, squeezing past a dining room table with one full set of chairs around it—and another dozen against the wall.

"She never used this room," Mrs. Scudpole assured us.

"Where did she eat?" I was curious enough to inquire.

"Wherever she liked."

"Where is the master bedroom?" I asked.

"Right at the end of the hall."

We went to the end of the hall and entered another used-furniture warehouse. Three

13

dressers, two toilet tables, and against the far wall, one hideous canopied bed. A second bed would not have gone amiss as both Miss Thackery and myself are accustomed to sleeping alone. Unless the second bed were to hang from the ceiling, however, there was no room for it in the bedchamber.

"That there bed belonged to Mrs. Siddons a dozen years ago," Mrs. Scudpole told us.

I lifted the fading gold coverlet and saw a set of sheets that might very well have been slept in by the aging actress a dozen years ago.

"Why did you not change the linen, Mrs. Scudpole? You knew we were coming."

"Nobody told me to."

"Would you please change the linen now," I said, quelling my temper. No doubt the linen closet held dozens of sheets seized from Thal's tenants.

"I shall call in a used-furniture dealer tomorrow," I said to Miss Thackery. "No one would buy the house in this condition. I must turn off the tenants as well, I daresay."

"Unless they have signed leases, of course," Miss Thackery said calmly. "You may be required by law to honor their leases. You will have to speak to Duggan about that."

"I shall hire my own solicitor. Duggan has not been very helpful. He did not tell me the house was full of tenants."

"If they are all as respectable as Mr. Alger, perhaps the new buyer would be happy to have them."

I had not forgotten Mr. Alger by any means. His was not an easy face to forget, but I was by no means sure of his respectability. While

Mrs. Scudpole changed the linen, Miss Thackery and I returned to the saloon. We had just taken a seat when a young woman appeared at the doorway.

"Good evening," she said in a good provincial accent, and curtsied. "I am Mrs. Clarke, from 2B. And you must be Miss Irving," she said to Miss Thackery.

We soon straightened that out, and I asked what she wanted. "I came to give you my month's rent, ma'am," she said. She peered to make sure we were alone, then added, "I could not like to give it to Mrs. Scudpole. We had thought the lawyer would come to collect it. Perhaps I should have sent it to him."

The girl was pleasant, and respectable in appearance. She was younger than myself. I judged her age to be about eighteen.

"Do you and Mr. Clarke live in 2B?" I asked, as she had introduced herself as Mrs.

"Oh no, Ma'am. I am a widow. My husband was killed in the Peninsula. He was an officer," she said proudly.

"I am very sorry to hear of his death."

"It was a great tragedy," she said sadly, "but at least I have little Jamie to bear me company. My son," she said, smiling softly. "It is difficult to raise him on my husband's pension, but I was fortunate to find a woman who looks after him while I work. That is Bea Lemon—Miss Lemon."

"What sort of work do you do, Mrs. Clarke?" Miss Thackery asked.

"I am a modiste," she said. "You would not think it to look at me, but I am quite good. I get it from my mama. She was French. Not that

15

I speak French myself," she added hurriedly, and looked to see that I did not think she was giving herself airs.

Indeed I would not have taken her for any of the things she claimed to be. She did not look like a widow or mother or French modiste. She looked like a yeoman farmer's young daughter, halfway up the ladder to becoming a lady. Her blond hair was arranged somewhat haphazardly about a pale but pretty face. Her eyes were blue, long-lashed, and had the glow of youth. But the girl looked tired, as well she might with the hard life she lived. One had to feel sorry for her, soldiering on alone to raise her little son.

"You won't be raising the rents, will you?" she asked timorously. "Mr. Butler mentioned it."

"Nothing has been decided. I shall very likely sell the house, Mrs. Clarke."

"Oh I wish you will not! Some horrid old rack-rent will buy it, and either turn it into a gin mill or raise the rents on us. I don't know what I shall do! It is so hard to find decent rooms within walking distance to the shop, and I cannot afford to hire a cab twice a day."

I felt extremely sorry for her, yet I could not base my whole future on the convenience of one poor widowed mother.

"We shall see," I said vaguely.

She looked at me with tears brimming in her big blue eyes. "I wish you will stay. You seem so nice." Then she lifted her fingers and wiped away the tears. "I'm sorry, Miss Irving. I would not ask it for myself, but for Jamie..."

I had a strong feeling Mrs. Clarke would face

lions or tigers for her son. "In any case, I shall try to help you find some other rooms if I decide to sell," I promised rashly.

She smiled sweetly and repaid me in the only way she knew. "You can come up and see Jamie tomorrow, if you like. He is sleeping now."

"Thank you, my dear. I should very much like to see him."

It was the first time I had ever called anyone "my dear." It made me feel old.

"He takes after his papa," she said, shyly but proudly. "I had a likeness of James taken before he left. It is such a comfort to me. Mr. Butler knows an artist who will make a copy on ivory, for me to wear as a pendant, but it costs a guinea."

"Won't you sit down, dear?" Miss Thackery said, as the girl seemed in a mood to talk— and we had nothing more demanding to do.

"I should be getting back upstairs. Would you mind giving me a receipt, Miss Irving? Mr. Butler said I should always get a receipt. Not that Mrs. Cummings ever tried to diddle us, but Mr. Butler was made to pay twice in a different establishment."

"Very prudent," Miss Thackery said approvingly.

"I am afraid I don't have a receipt book," I said. I felt a little annoyed that she did not trust me, but realized it was only my lack of business experience. The girl was right.

"In the middle drawer of the desk, Miss Irving," she said, nodding to one of many desks in the room. I found the receipt book and wrote out her receipt.

She was about to leave when another tenant

called. A decent-looking young gentleman came bowing in and announced he was Mr. Butler, the same fellow who took such a keen interest in the widow's affairs. He was of medium height, and decently appareled in day clothes. The buttons on his blue worsted jacket were several sizes larger than gentlemen wore in Radstock, but the jacket itself was well enough. He had bright brown eyes and reddish hair that curled in a way any lady would envy. His face looked the way a cherub's face might look after a few years of dissipation. Not that Mr. Butler looked dissipated, but he did look more harassed than a cherub.

He could not keep his eyes off the young widow. Until she darted back upstairs to Jamie, there was not much sense to be gotten from him. Once she had left, he turned to business.

"That is my month's rent, paid up right and tight. Scudpole was hinting for it, but I am not such a greenhead as to hand it over to *her*."

I wrote out his receipt without asking. "Do you have a lease for your flat, Mr. Butler?" I asked, as I was curious to know how soon I might be rid of my unwanted tenants.

"Eh? A lease? No. I daresay you are wondering why we pay by the month, instead of quarterly. Mrs. Cummings had no use for leases. She said she found it easier to boot unmannerly tenants out if they did not sign a lease. Are you planning to raise the rents? If you mean to go charging us more, the least you might do is have a light in the hallways at night. And fix those drafty windows. Mrs. Clarke tells me there is a regular gale blowing through her bedroom in the winter."

"I have no intention of raising the rents, Mr. Butler. I plan to sell the house, and am merely curious to know how much notice I must give the tenants."

"Demme! I don't know what poor Mrs. Clarke will do if you kick her out. It ain't every house that will take a child in. She has had a rough time of it, I can tell you."

"Are you and Mrs. Clarke old friends?" Miss Thackery asked. "From the same part of the country, is what I mean."

"No, I only met her six months ago. She is from Somerset. Can you not tell from her pretty accent? I am from Devonshire. My papa sent me to London to work upon 'Change, thinking I would make my fortune."

"What do you do upon 'Change?" Miss Thackery persisted.

"Mostly I do ciphering and write out fair copies of letters. It is demmed boring work, I can tell you, and there is no fortune in it, either, for us at the bottom of the pole. I am trying to get into Whitehall. So you say you are selling the house?"

"I am afraid so, Mr. Butler."

"I wish you would reconsider. I daresay we could all eke out a few more shillings for a higher rent, if that is—"

"No, it is not that," I said hastily.

I felt somehow responsible for the difficult lives of these youngsters. I noticed Mr. Butler had ink on his fingers, and the seat of his trousers was shiny from sitting on some stool, poring over columns of figures, or copying letters. I had not realized life was so very difficult for some people. My greatest hardship was Mrs.

19

Hennessey, and what did Papa's marrying her amount to in the end? I would have to share Miss Thackery's bedroom, and have to live with Mrs. Hennessey and her vulgar daughters. It was bad enough, but nothing to poor Mrs. Clarke and even Mr. Butler, who already looked haggard. He could not be much more than twenty or twenty-one.

And when I sold the house, their lives would be even more difficult. They would have to move into quarters even worse or more expensive than the ones they inhabited now.

Mrs. Scudpole shuffled to the doorway and said, "The bed's changed. I don't do laundry. These sheets will have to be sent out. You owe the laundress for the last wash."

"Make up an itemized list of the expenses owing, Mrs. Scudpole, and we shall go over it tomorrow."

She left without replying. Mr. Butler said, "You want to have a word with the laundress yourself. Old Scuddie is a famous cheat. Your aunt never trusted her with a penny. I do wish I could convince you to keep the house running. You will find it a very convenient location, I promise you. Close to Temple Bar and Mam'selle Lalonde's Modiste Shop and Drury Lane."

Neither Temple Bar nor Mam'selle Lalonde's shop was of much interest to me, and I knew from yesterday's drive through Long Acre that we were far removed from polite London. Wild Street had not a single thing to recommend it to me, but I did not go into that with Mr. Butler. He pocketed his receipt and left, secure of at least one more month's lodging in this decrepit paradise.

"Take a look in that receipt book and see who else owes for the month's rent, Cathy," Miss Thackery suggested.

I checked through the past month's stubs and saw that we were still to hear from a Professor Vivaldi (attic), a Miss Irene Whately (3A), Mr. Eric Sharkey (3B), and Mr. Alger (2A). Six tenants in all. Mrs. Clarke (2B) and Mr. Butler (3C) had already paid. After a little ciphering I had figured out my annual rents.

"Aunt Thal was making three hundred pounds a year on this hovel!" I exclaimed. I checked my arithmetic to see I had not erred. "That is more than the interest on my five thousand dowry. I get only two hundred and fifty on it. Surely these rents must be usurious!"

"It seems to me Mr. Butler and Mrs. Clarke think they are getting a bargain, or why would they be asking if you plan to raise the price?"

"I wonder what I could sell the place for? Perhaps it is worth more than I thought."

"We shall have an estate agent call tomorrow. If the new owner fixed it up, he could raise the rents and make himself a tidy fortune. You must bear that in mind when you sell, Cathy."

We discussed the matter for half an hour. Tomorrow we would arrange to have a builder tour the house with us to see that it was in solid condition as to roofs and rafters and so on. The next day, we would call in an estate agent and put it up for sale. And meanwhile, there were still those four rents to collect. They would help defray the cost of our visit.

After our strenuous day, we retired at ten o'clock, to spend a very uncomfortable night crowded two into a bed, listening to assorted troublesome noises in the street beyond. At Radstock, we were not accustomed to hearing carriages into the small hours of the morning, drunken revelry, loud talking, and even an occasional bloodcurdling scream, which Miss Thackery half convinced me was only caterwauling. I had no idea what the arrangements were for the locking of the front door. Did each tenant have his own key, or was it left open twenty-four hours a day? That was another thing to check in the morning. Eventually I slept.

Chapter Three

I spent an unsettled night. The timbers of the old house squeaked and squawked. Doors were opened and shut at all hours. Not just the front door the tenants used, but the back door as well. The noises from the kitchen area were not loud, however. If Mrs. Scudpole had visitors, she was at least quiet about it. Almost stealthy...

I finally slept, and was awakened by a pounding on the steps at seven o'clock the next morning. I lay for a moment with my eyes closed, wondering who could be making such a racket at the rectory. Then I felt an elbow prodding my back and remembered where I was—and why I had company in my bed. I opened my eyes and stared at the collection of used furnishings packed around the walls. I had forgotten that chore when Miss Thackery and I were discussing what we must do before selling the house. We must have someone in to remove this lumber. A close examination had proven it to be virtually worthless. With luck, the man would take the furniture as payment for removal, and we would get the job done without expense.

I lay quietly, for I did not wish to disturb my friend's slumber. My inheritance was a slum; my housekeeper was a slatternly cheat; I had several days' work ahead of me dealing with business people I was totally unequipped to deal with—and yet I was happy. Some festive air had attached itself to this unlikely holiday. It would give my quiet life a good shaking up to see how other people lived. Hopefully I would be a more understanding person as a result. But I doubted I would be generous enough to be happy with my new stepmama.

When Miss Thackery stirred to life, I rose and prepared for the day, giving her a few moments to collect her thoughts. The water in the basin was cold, but at least it was clean. I washed in it, and when I had dressed, I rang for Mrs. Scudpole. She did not answer the bell. Thinking she might be sweeping the stairs or performing some necessary chores about the house, I took the washbasin to the kitchen myself. The cold stove told me she was not yet up.

There was some commotion in the alley by the house. I went to the window to see what was afoot. A wagon, its load covered by a tarpaulin, was just pulling out. My alleyway was private property, and I went to the door to see who had been using it.

A disreputable-looking workman lifted his hat and said, "Good morning, miss." There was another man on the wagon as well. He was small, and had a hat pulled down over his eyes. I noticed he did not wear the fustian jacket of a workman, but a gentleman's blue worsted with big brass buttons.

"What are you doing here?" I inquired, politely but firmly.

"Just leaving, miss," the driver replied. "I lost my way, and used your alley to get my bearings. No harm done." He whipped up his bedraggled old jade and left.

The fellow was certainly up to no good. With so little traffic on the street, he could have stopped and taken his bearings there. I did not see what mischief he could have been doing in the alley, however, so I thought no more of it.

A door off the kitchen was open, showing me an unmade bed. I went in, but Mrs. Scudpole was not there. I thought she might have decamped on us, which would explain the noises coming from this area during the night. I half hoped she had left, but a second look showed me her clothing and personal effects were there. Perhaps she had dashed out to buy us fresh milk or eggs. I filled the basin and took it to Miss Thackery.

When she was dressed, we went back to the kitchen. There was still no sign of Mrs. Scudpole. We would have gone without breakfast were it not for Miss Thackery, who was raised on a farm and knows the trick of getting a fire going. We boiled water, boiled eggs, made tea, and had our meal with untoasted bread, as we could find no facilities for making toast. While we ate, the front door slammed a few times, but it must have been the tenants going out to work, because it was not Mrs. Scudpole returning.

At nine, she still had not come back, and we began to worry about her. I thought perhaps we should send for Bow Street. Miss Thackery came up with the more sensible suggestion of asking our tenants if they knew where she might be. We were about to go upstairs and start knocking on doors when Mrs. Scudpole straggled into the kitchen, still wearing her abominably soiled apron. She carried neither milk nor eggs, nor anything else, nor did she come from outside, but from the hall leading to our rooms.

"Where have you been?" I demanded.

"I fear I must have slept in."

"Indeed you did. It is after nine o'clock. We didn't know what had happened to you."

"Your aunt didn't get up so early."

"But you were not in your bedroom," I said.

A sly look came into her eyes and she replied, "Mrs. Cummings gave me the other bedchamber to use. She said it was all right. My mattress is as lumpy as a bag of stones."

"You mean there are two bedchambers besides your own! Why did you not tell us? Why did you not show me that room yesterday?"

"She said I could use it."

I may not be much good at business, but I know when a woman is lying. Her shifty eyes refused to meet mine. All her belongings were still in her own room. She had moved into that good room on her own.

"We shall require the second bedroom now, Mrs. Scudpole," I said coolly. "Naturally we shall expect clean linen. And as you only act on orders, I shall tell you to put on a clean apron and brush your hair. Miss Thackery and I rise

25

at seven-thirty. We take tea and eggs and toast for breakfast. Have you prepared that list of debts we spoke of last night?"

"I don't do ciphering. I've got it all in my head. If you just give me the money, I'll pay it."

"Give me the names of the people who are owed. I shall pay them myself."

She mentioned a local butcher shop and a Mrs. Lawson, the laundress. They appeared to be the only bills outstanding. In fact, after some sly comments about my aunt's unexpected death, she was not certain any money was owing at all, and *I* was morally certain it had all been a ruse to rob me.

"I shall personally handle all household finances in the future. After you have cleaned up yourself and this kitchen, I would like you to sweep and dust the front stairs, Mrs. Scudpole. We shall begin on the rest of the house after I have the excess lumber removed. It is impossible to clean with the house in this jumbled state."

On this haughty speech, I left the room, with Miss Thackery darting out after me. We went to examine the other bedchamber and found it the best room in the place. It was done in light oak furnishings, with seafoam green carpet and hangings. The walls were covered in a delicate Chinese paper with birds and flowers. The room had not been inundated with excess furnishings. In fact, I knew at a glance it was the bedroom my aunt had actually used, for her personal belongings were there. The toilet table held a large assortment of brushes and bottles and cosmetics. The clothespress was bulging with exotic gowns.

26

"Thal Cummings was always a clotheshorse," Miss Thackery said, as she sorted through the gowns. "There is some lovely material here, Cathy. And she was so big that there is plenty of it. We can make some of these over for you."

"Perhaps I shall pick out a few of them to take with me when I leave. Now, what should we do first? I believe we must be rid of the excess furnishings before we call in the builder to assess the building. He would not be able to see the walls and floors for all this stuff."

"Let us make a list," she suggested. Miss Thackery is a great one for making lists.

We went to the saloon and began itemizing what we must do. Before we had gotten far with it, there was a tap at the doorway, and an elderly gentleman came in. He was tall and lean, with pince-nez glasses and wispy gray hair. He looked like a retired cleric or schoolmaster. His clothing was of good quality, and he wore a gold watch, or at least a watch chain, but the clothes were shiny from prolonged wear.

"Ladies," he said, with a gallant bow. "I am Professor Vivaldi. I have come to pay the rent on the attic rooms." He had a slight trace of an accent. Italian, would it be, with a name like Vivaldi?

We introduced ourselves, and I got out the receipt book. Like the others, he paid in cash, and like the others, he inquired whether we meant to continue hiring rooms and at what rate. I told him what I had told the others. He seemed distressed and said "Pity," in a rather pathetic way, but he did not urge us to keep the house operating.

Then he rose and put on his curled beaver.

27

"I am off to the British Museum. A little work I am preparing on the antiquities in Greece," he explained. "I used to go there often during the summers when I was teaching at Oxford."

We watched from the window as he walked down the street. Here was another unfortunate soul to feel sorry for. I did not think we were very close to the British Museum, but perhaps Bloomsbury was closer than I realized. However far it was, that shiny jacket told me the professor would be walking, and at his age. A sad comedown for an Oxford professor.

After he had left, Miss Thackery and I discussed our tenants. We agreed that they were a cut above what one would expect to find in such a derelict neighborhood. A professor, an officer's widow, a young man working upon 'Change, and Mr. Alger, whose occupation we had not yet learned, but who gave the best appearance of the lot.

Within a few minutes, there was another clatter of footfalls on the uncarpeted stairs, followed by another tap at the door. My spirits lifted to see it was Mr. Alger who stood, waiting entrance. I do not mean that my heart fluttered in any silly, girlish way, although he was exceedingly handsome. What made me feel better was that he was one tenant who did not make me feel guilty. He looked prosperous, and well able to take care of himself. In short, he looked completely out of place on Wild Street.

"The day of reckoning is at hand," he said, entering with a bow and a teasing smile. I looked at him in alarm. "How foolish of me," he said, laughing. "I do not mean the biblical end of the world, but only rent day."

"I feel sure we would have had some har-binger if Armageddon was at hand," I replied.

His eyebrows lifted in surprise. His eyes examined me again, minutely. They strayed to Miss Thackery, a very pattern card of respectability, then settled down. When he spoke, his accent was more polite. "My rent is overdue, but with Mrs. Cummings's death, we hardly knew whom to pay."

I got out the receipt book. While I accepted the money and wrote out his receipt, Miss Thackery said, "Perhaps you can give us a little advice, Mr. Alger. We want to have all this excess lumber hauled away. Cathy—Miss Irving—thought a tranter might take the furnishings in lieu of payment."

He blinked in astonishment at such unbusinesslike goings-on. "What, *give* it away?" he asked. "Why do you not sell it?"

As it was my furniture, I replied, "I fear the price of hiring a wagon might exceed what I would make on selling the lumber. It is not fine furniture, Mr. Alger, but scratched and dented pieces, half with the knobs or handles off."

"Except for the Hepplewhite desk," Miss Thackery added.

Mr. Alger went to look over the assorted pieces in the saloon. He looked over his shoulder with a conning smile. "If the idea is not to make profit, but only to get the lumber out of your flat, I have a different suggestion to make."

"Let us hear it," I said.

"I believe your tenants would be happy to have the use of it. The rooms are advertised as 'furnished,' but they contain only the minimum. It is surprising how little furniture one can get along with. I could certainly make good use of one of these desks," he said, running his palm over the one good piece in the lot, the Hepplewhite desk. "And if there is a spare dresser or toilet table, I know Mrs. Clarke has been wishing she could afford some sort of chest for Jamie's things. That is her son."

"We have already met Mrs. Clarke," Miss Thackery said.

"A charming girl, and a sad case. We all take a parental interest in Mrs. Clarke," Alger said, with a soft smile.

Mr. Butler's interest could hardly be called 'parental,' and I was none too sure what hue Mr. Alger's interest took, but the widow was certainly pretty—and in need of any help she could find.

"I have no objection to the tenants making use of it if they like," I said at once.

"Then I claim this desk!" Alger said, placing his palm on the Hepplewhite. "I promise you I shall take good care of it."

"That one piece is fairly good," I said.

Miss Thackery cast a questioning look to see if I would let the Hepplewhite go. I consoled myself that the furnishings were only being lent to the tenants. "You can have the desk when I sell the house, if you want it," I told her.

"You are surely not planning to sell the house!" Mr. Alger exclaimed.

"This is not the sort of place we could live in," I assured him.

"It is not what you are accustomed to, I daresay. I don't believe Mrs. Cummings ever mentioned your circumstances... ?"

There was a question in his eyes. "We come

from Radstock. My papa is the rector there," I said.

"I see." The rapid blinking of his eyes and choked voice told me he had not expected such a genteel background. Having caught me dusting with a dirty face and apron yesterday, he had apparently taken me for a commoner.

"So you see, we could not possibly live here," I explained.

Mr. Alger looked at a seat. I nodded agreement to his occupying it, and he began to try to talk me out of selling.

"I expect life is quiet in Radstock," he said. "There is something to be said for tasting the various spices of life. I find Wild Street fascinating. You feel the very pulse of a large city beating all about you."

"Yes, and you hear and smell it, too," Miss Thackery said. "We could hardly sleep for the racket in the streets."

"One soon becomes accustomed to that," he informed us. "It is all part of the local color. And here in the theater district, you might meet all manner of interesting characters. I have found it a broadening experience."

"I find cutthroats and gin mills an experience I can do without," I replied.

"Indeed? I would have thought a rector's daughter might be interested in helping the less fortunate."

I blush to confess this notion had not so much as entered my head. Good works played a large part in my life, but they were such tame good works as supplying food to the hungry and organizing the church bazaars.

"I fear I am not qualified to help much in

31

this case. Wild Street is too..." I said uncertainly.

"Wild?" he suggested. "Perhaps you are right. You are too tame to tackle real poverty and need. The poor helpless women, forced on to the streets at an early age, the homeless children."

"You cannot expect me to single-handedly right the wrongs of London, Mr. Alger," I said sharply, for I did feel a few qualms of guilt at what he was saying.

"You are right. It is beyond one person. We must each do what we can— But you have a comfortable home elsewhere, of course. We cannot expect you to disrupt your life only because the people here are so needy."

I felt a perfect hypocrite. Was I being horridly selfish in running back to my comfortable life? Of course I did not tell him that my whole life was on the verge of disruption in any case. Miss Thackery intimated something of the sort, however.

"Miss Irving thought she might sell this place and hire a flat, perhaps in Upper Grosvenor Square. You may be sure she would involve herself in charitable works, Mr. Alger."

Mr. Alger's eyebrows rose in interest. "Then you are thinking of removing to London! How very nice." His smile suggested that he was delighted to hear it.

"As soon as the furniture is removed, I plan to have a man in to look the place over, to see it is in good repair."

"There is no need to do that," he said. "Whoever buys it will not care if the roof leaks. This is rack-rent territory, Miss Irving. The landlords squeeze the maximum number of people into the minimum of space, charge the poor wretches whatever the traffic will bear, take their money, and run. Not that I mean to traduce your aunt! As she lived here herself, she took more interest. I know the roof does not leak in any case. I drop in on Professor Vivaldi from time to time, and he is snug and dry."

"Then there is no need to waste your money on having an inspection, Cathy," Miss Thackery said.

"Yes, you are right. I dislike to think of my poor tenants falling into the hands of a rack-rent, but really—"

Before I could say more, Mr. Alger leapt on my innocent words. "The house is not at all a bad business investment, Miss Irving." He drew a chair up to mine and began to outline his meaning. Having failed to move me by pretending the neighborhood was interesting, or by guilt, he now pelted headfirst into appealing to my greed.

"You would be extremely fortunate to get five thousand for the place, and if you are in a hurry to sell, you would get more like four. I assume you would invest your capital in Consols?" I nodded. "Very well then, five percent of four thousand—two hundred pounds per annum. Your rents here amount to three hundred."

"But the house would cost at least fifty pounds a year to maintain. I would not be much further ahead."

"Au contraire!" he said, lifting his eyebrows in astonishment. "You are forgetting the entire ground floor, the most valuable part of the house. You can either live in it rent-free yourself, or rent it to someone for a hundred pounds a year. If you sell, you would have to hire rooms. In Upper Grosvenor Square, a flat of this size would cost considerably more than a hundred pounds. Rent is money down the drain. If you stay here, your house would be appreciating with inflation, and with the growth of London. Real estate is an excellent investment at this time. From the economical point of view, your best bet is to stay on here."

"I really cannot see myself and Miss Thackery living here," I said, "but as an investment, it might not be a bad thing. I shall think about it."

"The neighborhood is not so bad as you might think," Alger continued. He was a persuasive talker. "I wager your driver brought you via Long Acre, the worst possible route."

"Yes, we came via Long Acre."

"You should have come by the Strand. Why do I not show you the route now? My patron has given me the use of a carriage."

"Where do you stable it?"

"In your stable. Mrs. Cummings gave me permission. If you are wondering why the hire of the stable is not shown in my rent rate, I can explain."

"I was not checking up on you, Mr. Alger!"

He shook a shapely finger at me and laughed. "You should have been! If you are to become a business lady, you must keep track of the pennies, Miss Irving. The fact is, Mrs. Cummings liked to do a little barter on the side, to keep her income low for tax purposes. I pay for the stable by allowing her to use my carriage. When she wished to go out, I had it sent back from Whitehall. She occasionally used it in the evenings as well. Your aunt liked attending the theater."

"I have only my papa's traveling carriage, and it is cumbersome for city traffic. We might continue the former arrangement, Mr. Alger, if that suits you?"

"That suits me very well indeed." He smiled. "Did I mention I was often her escort?" A flirtatious smile accompanied this suggestion.

Miss Thackery had lit on a point of his conversation that I had missed. "What do you do at Whitehall, Mr. Alger?"

"Whitehall!" I exclaimed. "We thought you were an actor."

Alger said, "Good lord! Am I *that* bad?" and laughed.

"It is not a question of bad," Miss Thackery said. "It just did not occur to us that someone from Whitehall would deem Wild Street a proper place to live."

"Indeed I do. Would I recommend it to you, if I did not? To answer your question, ma'am, I am secretary to Lord Dolman. He is active in the Upper House. His particular area of expertise is trade. It is not an onerous position. At the next election, he wants me to stand for Parliament in his riding. I plan a political career. As you are wondering why I live here," he added uncertainly, "the fact is, I have a small annuity from my papa, but I am by no means independently wealthy. Until I have gained a few synecures at Whitehall, I must live more or less hand-to-mouth. Lord Dolman offered me rooms in his mansion on Berkeley Square, but I prefer a certain amount of independence. Lord Dolman is a connection by marriage," he added, to explain this lord's generosity.

Personally, I would have leapt at the rooms

in Berkeley Square, but I could understand a young gentleman wanting his independence.

His explanations finished, he said, "Are you free to have a little tour of the neighborhood now, Miss Irving?"

"We have a great many things to do this morning," I replied. But as I thought over our conversation, I saw there was really not that much to be done now. The tenants were to remove the furnishings; I was no longer going to hire a builder to inspect the premises; and until I had mulled over the advantages and disadvantages of selling the house, I would not call on an estate agent.

"I can stay and collect the rents from the other tenants, if you like," Miss Thackery offered. "And I shall ride herd on Mrs. Scudpole, too. Fancy her taking the best bedchamber, and letting on Thalassa slept in that warehouse of a room."

"I should do something about letting the tenants know they can have the excess furniture," I said.

"There is a billboard tucked under the staircase in the front hall," Mr. Alger informed me. "I suggest you set the hours when the furniture is available, or you will have folks landing in on you all day. You might want to oversee that the pieces are fairly distributed. Just so no one takes my desk," he said, glancing to the Hepplewhite.

"I shall post the notice," Miss Thackery said. "Shall we say this evening between eight and nine, so that everyone is home and gets an equal chance?"

I agreed to this time. There was nothing further

to detain us. I got my bonnet and pelisse and rejoined Mr. Alger in the saloon. Mrs. Scudpole, in a cleanish apron, was sweeping the front stairs. Mr. Alger stared at this unusual occurrence.

He said in heartfelt accents, "I really do wish you would stay on, Miss Irving. You could make something of this place."

"Perhaps you can talk me into it, sir, but first you must convince me it is not necessary to traverse Long Acre to get to the civilized part of town."

Chapter Four

With other matters to occupy my mind, I had given no thought to where Mr. Alger's groom lived, and how he was summoned when required. I soon learned there was no groom to worry about. Alger drove a sporting carriage, and after assisting me on to a perilously high perch, he hopped up and took the ribbons himself. I had never been in a curricle before. The daughter of a provincial cleric must be especially nice in her behavior. But as no one I knew would see me here, I planned to enjoy the outing.

"Lord Dolman must be a youngish gentleman," I said, as the dashing yellow curricle and lively team of grays clipped along.

"No, why do you say that?"

"Because of this curricle. When you spoke of wanting your independence, I thought he must be a crusty old fellow."

"He would be shocked to hear himself described in that way. He is well enough, but when you are a guest in a gentleman's house, you are at his beck and call. One's plans must be changed if an extra man is required for dinner or the theater."

"Surely that would not be much of an imposition!"

"That depends on what lady requires an escort. You may be sure it is not the Incomparables who lack a companion." He turned a conning smile on me. "I am a little particular about the ladies I squire about town."

I believe that was intended as a compliment, but there was a superficiality in it that irked me. "Not every lady is so fortunate as to be beautiful—nor does it matter in the least, so long as she is of good character."

"Only a lady sure of her own charms would say so." He smiled.

"Should you not be enlarging your circle of... prominent friends," I said, struggling over the proper word to describe the sort of people he would not meet on Wild Street, but that would be helpful to a struggling politician.

"I frequently complete Dolman's party of an evening, but I prefer to do it at my own pleasure, and with advance notice. I do have a life and friends of my own as well."

"Of course," I said, nodding as though in agreement. But I had to wonder what sort of life and friends these were, that he had to keep them secret from his patron. I felt if Mr. Alger were truly interested in advancing his career, he would be more conciliating to Lord Dolman.

The curricle was dashing along at a speed that played havoc with my bonnet and pelisse.

I had a good idea why Alger was setting such a dangerous pace and wished him to slow down.

"With the best will in the world and the fastest team, Mr. Alger, you cannot conceal that the area we are flying through is disreputable in the extreme. Look at that!" I exclaimed, pointing to a pair of derelicts staggering down the street at ten o'clock in the morning, drunk as lords.

"Would the rector's daughter like to stop and try her hand at reforming them?" he asked playfully. I glared. "We will soon be on the Strand," he said, and after several more blocks of extremely dangerous driving, we did reach the Strand with the carriage still intact. Mr. Alger was an excellent fiddler.

"You can slow down to sixteen miles an hour now," I said, straightening my bonnet and arranging my pelisse.

He turned north on to Piccadilly and drove at a normal pace up New Bond Street, where the ton were on the strut, rigged out in the highest jet of fashion. I could not restrain a few gurgles of delight.

"So this is New Bond Street, that I have read of in *La Belle Assemblée*. And there is the very bonnet that was in last month's issue! Is it not charming? I wonder what shop carries it."

"A cut above the High Street in Radstock, eh, Miss Irving?" He smiled, happy to have found something to impress me at last.

"This beats even Milsom Street, in Bath," I breathed.

"High praise indeed!"

Several fashionable ladies and gentlemen nodded or waved to Alger. One pretty young lady with blond hair and a fetching high poke bonnet had her rig drawn to a stop and called, "I did not see you at Lady Bingham's rout last night, Algie. You promised me a waltz."

"We shall remedy that at the next rout," he called back. Then he drove on. "That was Miss Carter," he said.

The name meant nothing to me, but the face would recommend itself to any gentleman with eyes in his head. He did not stop to converse with any of the people who greeted him, nor did he heed my hint that the shops looked lovely.

I continued gawking about at the various bow windows holding elegant trifles, and the crowds jamming the street. "I have never seen so many people, even in Bath," I said.

"To us in London, going to Bath means rusticating. I wager you will feel the same after you have become accustomed to the pleasures of London. The theaters, the balls, the routs."

An elegant young gentleman took his life in his hands to cross the street in the middle of heavy traffic. "I say, Algie, are you going to the club this evening?" he called.

"Not tonight, Pelham. I am busy."

The man called Pelham turned his saucy grin in my direction. "I see." He grinned in a way that suggested I was to be the evening's entertainment. Then the exigencies of traffic caused him to dart off, to avoid being run down by another curricle.

"That was Lord Harding," Mr. Alger said. "But we were discussing your remaining in London, and the many entertainments available here."

I felt I was missing an opportunity to meet the very sort of people who could make those entertainments possible. My reply had a sharp note. "I do not anticipate such diversions as you speak of. I am hardly making my debut, you must know. In fact, I am in mourning."

"You are not wearing mourning clothes," he pointed out.

"Well, I never actually met Mrs. Cummings. Papa did not feel it necessary to go to the expense— That is—"

"I understand. As you do not consider your aunt close enough that you must wear mourning, some modest entertainments are not out of the question."

"If I remain, Miss Thackery and I shall hire modest rooms somewhere. I do look forward to the theaters and art galleries and libraries and drives."

"We shall go to the exhibition at Somerset House one afternoon when the carriage and I are free. You must not hesitate to tell me when you want it. That was our bargain."

The offer put me back in humor. "That would be lovely!"

Since Alger seemed reluctant to stop the carriage and take a walk, I felt he was in a hurry to get to work. I said, "Will Lord Dolman not expect you to be at the office by now?"

"He never goes to the House before noon."

"London is very strange. Men do not go to work before noon; my aunt did not rise until midmorning; she did not eat in her dining room."

"I told you the experience would be broadening." He laughed. "I got caught up on all my work before I left yesterday. About the balls, Miss Irving, I understand your reluctance to attend them, but I am invited to many less formal routs. If you have a taste for dancing, that aspect of London is by no means closed to a young lady who has not made her debut."

"You are very kind, but I did not come prepared for that sort of socializing. Papa expects me to put the house up for sale and return to Radstock within the week."

"But you mentioned hiring a flat in town," he said, looking a question at me.

"Yes, well, Papa does not know that yet," I confessed. "Until I have the money from the house, I am not in a position to remove from the rectory."

"So you do have some rebel blood in your veins. Good! Just what is it you have against your father's house, if it is not overly inquisitive of me to ask?"

Alger had driven back down New Bond Street to Green Park. It was sparsely populated at that early hour. Then, when there were no interesting young people to meet and no shops to look at, he suggested we get out of the carriage and walk. As we made a leisurely tour of the park, I found myself explaining about Mrs. Hennessey and her daughters.

"It all sounds very trivial and selfish after hearing how poor Mrs. Clarke and Mr. Butler live, but like you, I want some independence, Mr. Alger. I will never have it in Papa's house after he is married."

"Under the circumstances, I should do the same thing," he said at once. "But being a hard-headed businessman, I would stay on at Wild Street until the property had increased in value—and I had stored up a nest egg. Then I would hire a small house in the fashionable part of London."

"And how would you make any decent friends, living in Wild Street?" I asked. "One could hardly invite the gentry to dinner in that place."

"This is London. You would be surprised what oddities are overlooked here when a lady has a substantial dowry, ma'am."

"I do not have a substantial dowry. I have only five thousand pounds."

"And another five on the Wild Street property at today's prices. That makes ten thousand, the going price for a baronet. If you waited a few years to sell, your fortune would be more like fifteen thousand. We gazetted fortune hunters usually allow a little something for a lady's appearance as well." He stopped walking and let his eyes make a slow tour of my face, which I could feel turn pink as his admiring gaze lingered. "A face like yours, neither haggard nor short of teeth, no squint, no spots— Why your worth is closer to twenty thousand. I daresay the dukes will be falling all over you."

I said primly, "Don't be foolish."

"Why not? It is delightful to be foolish on a fine spring day… with a lovely lady by your side. And before you leap to some derogatory conclusion, let me say, I was not fooling about your being beautiful. You are, you know, in an unconscious sort of way."

"I am not unconscious!"

"You twist everything I say. I meant you were unconscious of being attractive."

"My hair is mousy."

"Tawny, like a lion's mane. Your eyes are rather lionlike, too. Green, with that peculiar slant."

"But lions do not have freckles."

"No, nor do they argue with every word a man says. I am trying to compliment you."

"Thank you, Mr. Alger. You are very handsome, too. In a few years, however, my face will devalue."

He gave me a laughing look. "Perhaps you should strike while the iron is hot—if you could be satisfied with a baronet, that is to say."

"And if a baronet could be satisfied to live on Wild Street. I assume these gazetted fortune hunters do not possess a home of their own to take a bride to."

"That is the luck of the draw, ma'am. But I think your face will hold together for a decade or more yet. You cannot be over twenty."

"I am one and twenty."

"Then you worry for nothing. I can give you ten years, and I still consider myself quite a stripling."

"Just so, but dogs and ladies age more quickly."

"I shall refrain from commenting on that incendiary speech." He put his hand on my elbow, and we resumed our walk. "More importantly, what do you think of my idea of remaining on at Wild Street? If it is the lack of friends, I might be of some help."

I had seen for myself that Mr. Alger had a good many friends. The notion was certainly tempting—but still, to live at Wild Street... "I shall think about it. Of course I would have to write Papa and see what he has to say."

"I shall be waiting to hear his reply. And for the meanwhile, you must not let the tenants take advantage of you, Miss Irving."

"I am not accustomed to being taken advantage of, Mr. Alger," I replied. His eyes narrowed as he tried to determine whether there was any reference to himself in that remark. "I notice Miss Whately and Mr. Sharkey have not yet paid their rent. I shall dun them this very evening." He did not reply, but I sensed some mischief lurking in the depths of his gray eyes. "The tenants seem very nice," I said. "I was surprised they were so respectable."

"Why thank you, ma'am. We try to behave ourselves."

"Oh, I did not mean you, Mr. Alger!" I said, laughing. Yet he was one of my tenants. After having spent an hour in his company, I could not fathom why he did stay at Wild Street. He was so obviously a cut above the others. He was even connected by marriage to the nobility. Surely there must be some reason why he did not live in a more gracious neighborhood. But he seemed extremely eager to talk me into keeping the house, and he certainly implied that he would continue as a tenant.

"Would a set of rooms at Albany cost much more than your rooms at my place?" I asked. "Mr. Nugent, a gentleman friend from Radstock, stayed there when he was in London a few years ago. He mentioned it was a favorite haunt of bachelors."

"Yes, it would cost much more," Alger said firmly. "Above my touch, I fear." Then he gave me a conning smile and said, "You sound as if you are trying to be rid of me, Miss Irving. I

45

hope the perilous pace I set in my curricle has not given you the notion I am a ramshackle fellow."

"No, it merely failed to conceal that the neighborhood is ramshackle, but I shall think over what you said. Very likely Papa will order me to sell the house and return at once."

"And will the rebel do as her papa orders?"

"Yes, I expect so. But when—if—he marries Mrs. Hennessey, I shall definitely remove to either Bath or London."

"I shall take you home now, to let you write your letter. Let us settle on a time to visit Somerset House. Are you free tomorrow afternoon?"

"What about your work?" I parried.

"I shall go to work in the morning instead. Dolman will be in committee meetings all afternoon. He shan't need me."

"That sounds like a convenient sort of position you have."

"I am not complaining," he replied airily.

"I should think not. Very well then, tomorrow afternoon."

We went back to the curricle and returned to Wild Street. Prepared for the worst, I found the house did not look so horrid as I remembered. If it had been on a more respectable street, with the windows cleaned and the door painted, it could have looked respectable, if not elegant.

Mr. Alger saw me to the door before returning to his curricle and presumably to Whitehall. That door filled me with revulsion. Successive layers of paint had cracked until the surface was the consistency of small curd. It is impossible to describe its color. I think the last coat of paint may have been black or gray, but it had a sort of iridescent haze to it that changed color with the passing shadows. It was so filthy that I handled the doorknob with care.

Mrs. Scudpole had prepared an indifferent lunch of more cold mutton and cheese.

"We cannot expect her to cook and clean and do everything," I said apologetically to Miss Thackery. "If Papa agrees to my remaining on awhile until we sell the house, we must hire more help. And of course we must send back his carriage, too."

I wrote the letter that afternoon, outlining the state of affairs here, and the potential profit if I held on to the house for a few years and did some minor repairs. Mullard posted the letter for me. He did not complain, exactly, but I took the notion that he was bored to flinders.

"P'raps you could find some odd jobs for me around the place, Miss Irving. The backyard could be made into a tidy little garden, if the rubbish was cleared away."

Miss Thackery and I went to the yard with him to survey it. If the interior of the house resembled a furniture warehouse. the outside was nothing else but a refuse heap. Any lumber my aunt felt not worth keeping had been unceremoniously dumped here. Broken chairs were heaped on top of a derelict stove, turning to rust. A wooden box was overflowing with broken crockery. The excess littered the ground.

"I could chop up those rotting chairs and whatnot and burn them in the stove or grate," Mullard suggested. "An ironmonger might haul away the old stove, and I could bury the crockery."

Miss Thackery, who was a gardener, thought we could grow vegetables in half the yard, with flowers in the other half.

"There were flowers here, once upon a time," she said, poking amid the debris. "Those are the leaves of peonies, and surely that is a rose-bush. It has thorns, but no flowers.

It was agreed that Mullard would begin cleaning up the yard. I went again and looked at the front of the house. A fresh coat of paint on the door would be an inestimable improvement. But first the curds of paint would have to be scraped or burned off. After careful consideration, we set upon dark green as a suitable color. A lighter shade would have been prettier, but the house did not lend itself to prettiness. As Miss Thackery said, with so many people using the door, and using it so carelessly, every kick mark and dirty fingermark would show up.

"I shall buy a nice brass knocker," I said, smiling to myself to think how fine this would look. "I shall ask Mr. Alger to take me to a shop when we go to Somerset House tomorrow."

I had told Miss Thackery of the proposed outing and asked her to join us. I did not like to leave her alone again.

We spent the remainder of the afternoon looking over the excess lumber indoors and putting little white stickers on those pieces that the tenants might help themselves to.

"We shall dun Mr. Sharkey and Miss Whately for their rent when they come to help themselves to the furniture," Miss Thackery said. "It is strange, I have not seen either one of them all day. I daresay Mr. Sharkey has been at work, but I wonder what Miss Whately does with herself."

Tapping footsteps sounded in the hallway. "That would be her," Miss Thackery whispered. We both looked expectantly to the door.

Chapter Five

The dainty tapping called up an image of a petite lady, perhaps elderly, refined. What stood framed in the doorway was a female of generous proportions, although the word "fat" did not immediately come to mind. Her flowing bosom and flaring hips, accentuated by a small waist, might have been painted by Rubens. Her white arms were dimpled at the elbows. She was not young, but not yet old, either. She could not by the wildest stretch of the imagination be called refined. Her ornately arranged coiffure and the quantity of paint on her face were enough to cast suspicions on her profession. Throw in the low-cut gown of violet silk, liberally sprinkled with bows, flowers, lace, buttons, brooches, and a wilted corsage of red roses, and you will know to what ancient profession I refer.

The vision opened its mouth, and a beautiful, throaty voice issued forth. I had been expecting something like the raucous caw of a jackdaw.

"Miss Irving," she said, billowing forth in full rig, accompanied by a strong aroma of violet scent. "I am Miss Whately, of 3A." She drooped to the floor in a curtsy that would have pleased old Queen Charlotte, for it was a very model of antique grace. She rose and smiled. "I am ever so pleased to make your acquaintance. I am just a little late with my rent. So sorry, dearie, but you wasn't here till yesterday. Better late than never, says I."

So saying, she handed me over her rent. An assortment of paste stone rings decorated her shapely white fingers. I thanked her and reached for the receipt book. Miss Thackery stood staring as if she had never seen anything like Miss Whately, and I am sure she had not. She was a type never seen in Radstock or Bath, unless on the stage. Her lovely voice, her graceful movements, and her living so close to Drury Lane made me wonder if she was an actress.

"You won't be closing up the house on us, will you Miss Irving?" was her first question.

I made the same reply I had made to the others.

"Lud, wouldn't that be just my luck!" she exclaimed, throwing a hand to her brow in a gesture of high melodrama. "Me just around the corner from Drury Lane. I knew it was too good to last."

Miss Thackery cleared her throat and said, "Are you an actress, Miss Whately?"

The question called forth another of the burlesque curtsies. Miss Thackery looked helplessly to me and returned a lesser curtsy. Miss Whately drew a chair forward and sat down, saying, "That I am, ma'am."

I introduced Miss Thackery, and Miss Whately said, "Listen, ladies, if you're planning to go to the theater, I can get you a deal on your tickets—same as I did for your aunt, Miss Irving. You'd ought to have seen *The Provok'd Husband*. I played Lady Wronghead. They wanted me to

50

play Lady Wronghead's daughter, because of my youth, you know, but it's a minor role. I had some wonderful scenes with Count Basset. Des Maitland played the count. He's a wonderful actor."

"Is it still playing?" I asked, with some interest.

"Lud no. That was last winter."

"What part are you playing at the moment, Miss Whately?" Miss Thackery asked.

"I'm at liberty just now, resting up after a very busy season. Parts are harder to come by since they got the new manager over to Drury Lane—Mr. Baker. He's got them all playing double roles for single pay! Tight as a fiddle string! Ask anyone. Baker wouldn't give you a sneeze if he had the flu. He wants me for *The Provok'd Wife*—it's like a companion piece to *The Provok'd Husband*. Vanbrugh is a wonderful dramatist."

"I thought perhaps you were on your way to the theater," Miss Thackery said, looking in confusion at the woman's costume.

"What? This old thing?" Miss Whately asked, and laughed a beautiful silvery laugh. "Lud, Miss Thack'ry, I wouldn't be caught dead on the stage in this old rag. No, Colonel Stone is taking me out to dinner tonight. He has been giving me a hurl in his carriage for a few weeks now. He's an old scarecrow, but a lady has got to eat, hasn't she? And there is no vice in him. He is well past it."

I blinked in astonishment at this plain speaking. To cover the stretching silence I said, "Did you happen to see the notice on the bulletin board, Miss Whately?"

"Not an increase in our rents!" she exclaimed.

"No, it is about furniture for the flats."

"Oh, lud, it's about that chair, ain't it? It was Sharkey who busted it, miss. If you're taking to charging us for busted furnishings, it's Sharkey you want to get after."

Miss Thackery handed her a slip of paper. "This is the notice," she said. She had apparently made a few efforts before being satisfied with her work and gave Miss Whately one of the rejects.

Miss Whately frowned at it for a moment. "Would you mind reading it for me, Miss Thack'ry. I've left my specs upstairs."

The white of her cheeks surrounding the rouge spots disappeared. It had turned as pink as the rouge, and I was struck with the idea that she could not read. How on earth did she learn her lines?

"The announcement says that I wish to be rid of the excess furnishings and invites the tenants to help themselves," I explained.

"I could use a decent dresser and an extra couple of chairs," she said, frowning. "How much are you charging?"

"There is no cost," I said. "The furniture is not needed here. It is only on loan. I will expect it to be left behind when the tenants leave."

"You mean it's *free*?" she said, her eyes bulging in disbelief. She leapt from the chair and darted to the edge of the room. "What are these little white bits of paper?"

"Those are the pieces I wish to have removed."

"I'll take this one," she said, snatching a little chest from the pile. "Just what I need to hold

52

my dainties. And a dresser, as I said, and half a dozen chairs. Say, you wouldn't have scrap of carpet, would you?"

I looked at the three under our feet. One was all the saloon required. "After the furnishings are removed, we shall see what we have here," I told her.

"I'll have Jack stay and give me a hand moving the stuff upstairs. That's Colonel Stone. On t'other hand, I don't want him to stick his fork in the wall before he buys me dinner. Can you just put my name on these pieces—and hold a slice of carpet for me, Miss Irving?"

"Yes, we can do that," I agreed.

The front door opened, and a shuffling sounded in the hallway.

"That'll be the colonel," Miss Whately said. "Yoo-hoo, Jack. In here," she called.

A doddering old relic of a gentleman shuffled in. He had snow white hair and a lined face. Miss Whately could have picked him up with one hand and lifted him over her head. I did not fear her virtue was in any danger from his advances.

He wore an evening suit of excellent cut. His accessories—gloves, watch chain, and a fine ruby in his cravat—suggested he was well to grass. He also behaved like a gentleman.

"Renie, my dear, charming as ever," he said in a quavering voice.

"This here is Miss Irving and Miss Thack'ry," Miss Whately said. The old colonel bowed punctiliously. "Charmed, ladies. Well, my dear, I hope you are in good appetite. I have reserved us a private room at the Clarendon—and ordered plenty of oysters, just as you like."

53

Miss Whately gave us a proud little look, as if to say, See how I have him trained? "Time for fork work," she said. "You won't forget about my furniture, Miss Irving? Just set it aside, or ask Sharkey to take it up for me. You have a key to my flat, of course."

"No, actually..."

"Scuddie has taken them, then. I would get hold of them if I was you, Miss Irving. If anyone is stupid enough to leave cash in his rooms, she'll pocket it, sure as shooting. Lud, what we poor working girls have to put up with," she said to her colonel, with a wild batting of her lashes.

"I wish you would let me take you away from all this, my little flower," he quavered.

"Now, Jack, you know your wife would skin you alive." She laughed merrily and took him out, bolstering him up on one side with her own strong body. "Ta ta, ladies. We must be stepping."

Miss Thackery and I sat in stunned silence a moment. What would the stylish Clarendon Hotel make of that woman? "I shall get the keys from Mrs. Scudpole," I said, and went after her.

She was in the kitchen, preparing dinner. She parted with the key ring reluctantly. I hoped I would not hear complaints from my tenants of cash or valuables missing from their rooms.

"I see Renie has found a new patron," Mrs. Scudpole said sourly.

I ignored the word "patron," although I feared it was accurate enough. "She is dining with Colonel Stone," I said.

"Hmph. Dining, is it? How does she manage to pay her rent and deck herself out in silks

54

and satins? She has not had a role for five years."

"You are mistaken. She played in a comedy last winter."

"Aye, for an audience of one at a time. She has not acted on the stage since I have been here—and that was five years this month. There is another word for what she does. Trollop!"

I took the keys and left. Miss Whately was the sort of tenant I had originally expected to be living in such a house as this, so I ought not to have been surprised. The relative gentility of the others had raised my expectations. At least she had paid her rent, and she was quiet. There remained only the elusive Sharkey to meet. Miss Whately's tale of his chair breaking did not lead me to hope for much from him.

For the next hour, the front door was often slammed. Mrs. Clarke and Mr. Butler returned, not together, but within minutes of each other. She was still reading the bulletin board when he came in, and we overheard their excited exclamations about the "free" furniture. Professor Vivaldi came in more quietly. Mr. Alger, having gone to work so late, did not return before dinner. We changed for dinner, but took no great pains with our toilette as the evening might involve some physical labor in the disbursement of the furnishings.

Mrs. Scudpole had exerted herself to roast a stringy, dry chicken and boil potatoes and peas to a mush.

"I shall tackle a small roast myself tomorrow," Miss Thackery said. "How on earth did she manage to ruin a fresh chicken? This tastes as if it has been in the oven a week."

"The wings and legs are hard as rocks. The

55

breast is edible. If we stay, we must hire someone who can cook. I am a little concerned about
Mr. Sharkey, Miss Thackery. We have not seen
a sign of him in over twenty-four hours. I mean
to call on him after dinner. I hope nothing has
happened to him."

"With luck, he will have absconded—without paying his rent."

"If so I shall try to get someone genteel to
take his rooms. That will leave only Miss Whately
to give the place a bad reputation."

"Why, you sound as if you intend to stay,
Cathy!" I did not deny it. I was beginning to
take a proprietarial interest in my tenants, and
in my horrid house. "I daresay we can thank
Mr. Alger for this idea," she suggested, with
an arch look.

"Don't be ridiculous," I scoffed, but I felt a
blush warm my cheeks. I found, too, that I kept
listening for the slamming of the front door,
heralding his return. When dinner was over, he
had still not come back, nor had Mr. Sharkey
appeared. It was seven-thirty, and we went to
the saloon to be ready to greet the tenants, come
to claim the lumber.

Chapter Six

I should enjoy being a shopkeeper, to judge by
that evening's work. It was amusing with customers coming in, outlining their requirements,
and making their selection. Everyone's favorite tenant was Mrs. Clarke, and she was given
precedence in selecting what she required for
Jamie. Her wants were modest: a chest of draw-

ers to hold the baby's clothing and blankets. She had a good eye in her head, too. She chose a piece of a pretty shape, saying, "Would it be all right if I painted it, Miss Irving? Jamie's coverlet is blue."

Mr. Butler, who followed a step behind her like a lady's footman, lent his support. "A lick of paint and it will be good as new. Miss Irving will not object to that."

Miss Irving did not object, but in fact pointed out a matching set of hanging shelves that might likewise be given a lick of paint and provide a display shelf for Jamie's toys.

Mr. Butler's eyes were busy spying out other treats for his beloved. It did not take a mind reader to see he was mad for the girl.

"You could use another chair, Anne," he said, examining the collection of chairs. "When Miss Lemon has tea with us, we have to bring the chair in from the bedroom."

"By all means have a chair. Have two," Miss Thackery said eagerly. Chairs were what we had most of.

With a little urging, Mrs. Clarke selected two chairs, and Mr. Butler took not less than three. I am sure I don't know what he meant to do with so many of them. While I tended the widow, Professor Vivaldi roamed the room and selected a desk and chair for himself. Mrs. Scudpole was not to be left out of anything that was free and was snapping up odd tables and assorted bric-a-brac.

Mullard was on hand to help bring the extra furnishings from the cluttered bedroom and move various pieces about, so the tenants could get a look at what was under or behind them.

We had the hallway quite full of lumber. Miss Lemon, afraid she was missing something, came downstairs carrying Jamie. She was a respectable, middle-aged woman who treated Mrs. Clarke with some strange mixture of a mother's bossiness, a maid's servility, and a friend's genuine concern.

"Jamie woke up, Mrs. Clarke," she said, "so I thought there was no harm in bringing him down. You know he likes a little romp before settling in for the night. You recall I wanted a bedside table and lamp, if there are any to spare."

Mrs. Clarke took the child to allow her nurse (or whatever Miss Lemon was) to roam the shop unencumbered.

Jamie was all an officer's son should be. His fat little face was topped by a fluff of dark curls. He had big blue eyes. Fresh from his nap, he was all smiles and gurgles. Miss Thackery and I admired him to his mama's satisfaction. We agreed he had his mama's eyes—and took her word for it that he had his papa's hair and ears.

"This is his birthday," Mrs. Clarke explained. "He is nine months old today. I made him this blue dress he is wearing."

It seemed strange to speak of nine months as a birthday, but the child loomed so large in her life that I expect he had a dozen birthdays a year. The dress was very well sewn, with ducks embroidered in yellow around the neck.

While I was admiring the dress, Mr. Alger returned and entered with good grace into the furniture business. The crowd shifted, and Professor Vivaldi came forward to admire Jamie.

"Is my Hepplewhite desk still here?" Mr. Alger asked.

"Indeed it is. You are welcome to a chair to go with it. We have a special on chairs this evening. Mullard has counted up an even two dozen of them to be disposed of."

"I shall strike a deal with you. Throw in a lamp, and I'll take two chairs off your hands."

"Clap hands on a bargain. Come into the hall. There is a matched set of walnut chairs there. Some of them even have four legs. They will set off the desk admirably, but I am not responsible if they fail to hold your weight."

While we were examining the walnut chairs and testing them for sturdiness of legs, the front door opened, and a little gnome of a man with kinky brown hair popped in. He was shorter than average but not actually a dwarf. I judged him to be a couple of inches shorter than my own five feet and four inches. He had brown eyes set deep in a pale, pudgy face with a day's growth of whiskers decorating it. His clothing was not only poorly cut but far from clean. His jacket had large brass buttons, padded shoulders, and a nipped waist that ill suited his build. His cravat had what looked suspiciously like drops of dried blood on it. But it was his frightened expression that lent him the air of a fugitive. He looked all around at the crowd, as if expecting someone to draw a pistol.

"Good God, who is that?" I exclaimed.

"You have not yet met Mr. Sharkey?" Mr. Alger said, smiling at my alarm. "Allow me to make you acquainted with your tenant."

Mr. Sharkey worked his way toward us. "What the deuce is going on, Alger?" he demanded. "Are the bailiffs in the house?"

Mr. Alger introduced us and explained the situation.

"You mean we can take what we want for free?" he demanded, his face a perfect picture of greedy incredulity.

"I am allowing the tenants the use of the items with a white tag," I said. He darted off to see what he could get.

"Don't forget to dun him for his rent," Mr. Alger reminded me, then he went to admire Jamie.

I went after Mr. Sharkey and found him in the saloon. He was not selecting furnishings, but stood at a little table of knickknacks that I wished to be rid of. The table held cheap, chipped statuettes, cracked ornamental bowls and vases, some imitation brass candlesticks, a mantle clock that had no hands, and such useless items.

"Can I have these?" he asked.

"Certainly, Mr. Sharkey, if you think you have room for them all. About your rent..."

He grabbed my sleeve and pulled me to a darkish corner. "Just what I wanted to speak to you about, Miss Irving. I can give you half on account. Business is slow at the moment— I'm having trouble collecting from some of my customers. You're a businesswoman yourself, and a very handsome one, if I may say so. You know how it is." His lips opened in a scheming smile that reminded me of a crocodile.

"Yes, indeed," I said, with a sagacious look.

"Heh-heh. I am good for the money. Ask anybody. I always pay Alger back."

"What business are you in, Mr. Sharkey?"

"I'm a wholesale dealer in odd-lot goods."

"Oh." I blinked in confusion.

"Let me explain." He seemed to find explaining easier with his short fingers clutching my sleeve. "I deal in bankrupt goods. Buy in job lots from stores that have gone bankrupt and sell to other stores. I deal in private residences as well—death sales mostly. A pity you hadn't spoken to me before giving away this lot," he said, waving a hand at the collected lumber. "I would have hauled it away for you. I have my own wagon. I could have gotten you a little something for it."

I looked at the large brass buttons, glowing dully in the dim light, and knew where I had seen them before. "Was that your wagon in the alley by my house this morning?"

"I got back late last night. I pulled it in there. I hope you don't mind."

"I mind that your driver did not tell me the truth when I inquired. In future I would prefer that you park elsewhere. If I, or Mr. Alger, wanted to use the alley, it would be inconvenient for it to be blocked."

"A good point. I'll speak to my driver. Now about the rent. I can give you half now... and the other half before next week. A deal?" The grubby hand came out to snatch mine.

"I suppose I can let you have until next week," I said, pulling my hand back. With any other tenant I would not have hesitated, but there was such a raffish air about Mr. Sharkey that I did not trust him an inch.

His pudgy face creased into a smile that displayed a set of small, dim teeth. "I knew you'd be reasonable. Listen," he continued, grabbing at my sleeve again. "If you need anything in

61

the way of personal gewgaws, come to me before you buy. I can get anything at a bargain. Ask Alger, or Butler. I got Butler a dandy gold watch at sixty percent off. I often come into such items in my line of business."

"I have very little need for gewgaws."

"I happen to have a dandy little garnet ring on me at the moment," he said. His hand went into his pocket and out came a ring with a red stone. He shoved it at me. I took it and examined it. It looked well enough. "I was saving this for my mama," he said, piercing me with a conning eye to see if I swallowed this unlikely story. "I could let you have this in lieu of the month's rent, if—"

"I would prefer cash, thank you, Mr. Sharkey."

He took the ring back and drew out a lady's watch. "How about this?" he asked, dangling it before my eyes.

It was a handsome thing. I had no need of another watch, but Miss Thackery had lost hers at a whist drive a year ago. When she recovered it the next day, it was smashed beyond repair.

"Where did you get it?" I asked.

"It came with the contents of a private house I bought up in Kent recently. That's where I have been the past few days, in Kent."

I took the watch to the lamplight. It was gold, or at least it looked like gold. The hinged lid was engraved with flowers, and the face was white enamel with a tiny wreath of roses hand-painted around the edge.

"This looks valuable, Mr. Sharkey. I fear it is worth more than one month's rent."

"Let's say two months then, and I am paid up in advance."

"I should warn you, I may not keep the house open for two months. I am thinking of selling."

"You can pay me the difference if you leave. I trust you," he said, with a greasy smile. "You'd be doing me a favor, Miss Irving. The fact is, I'm a little tight at the moment."

"I suppose it would be all right," I said. I did not feel quite right about it, but could see no actual harm in the transaction.

"We'll just keep it between ourselves," he said. "If the others hear, they'll all be wanting a bargain from me."

Professor Vivaldi came to inquire about a small table for his bedside, and I left Mr. Sharkey to look over what remained of the furnishings. In the hallway, plans were underway for the removal of the lumber.

Butler and Alger had each taken an end of Mrs. Clarke's chest of drawers, Miss Lemon carried Jamie, and I offered to help Mrs. Clarke with the hanging shelves. I own I was curious to see the rooms I was renting. Mrs. Clarke had her parlor done up in a simple but pretty way. The walls were painted a dull mustardy color, and the furniture was shabby, but she had contrived to brighten the room with cushions and pictures and those little touches that an artistic woman without much money can always invent. The old wooden pieces gleamed from assiduous polishing.

She thanked me three or four times and offered me tea, but I wished to oversee the removal of the rest of the lumber and returned below. Mr. Alger and Butler came as well, to carry up the chairs I had managed to palm off on the widow.

We met Professor Vivaldi and Sharkey on the stairs. Sharkey was helping the professor with his loot. Soon Sharkey returned below and began collecting the broken bibelots into a cardboard box.

"Can I have a word with you, Alger?" he called from the saloon, and Mr. Alger joined him.

I took an occasional peek into the saloon while reminding Butler which chairs were to go up to Mrs. Clarke's flat. I saw Sharkey showing Alger the ring with the red stone, and Mr. Alger shaking his head. Alger did not take the ring, but I believe Sharkey managed to either sell him something else or dun him for a loan, for Alger's wallet came out of his pocket, and bills changed hands. When Sharkey went bouncing upstairs, he wore a smile on his pudgy face.

"You have done pretty well, Miss Irving," Alger said, returning to the hallway. "When I get my desk and chairs out of your way, you will have room to swing a very small kitten in here."

"Make that a cat. Miss Whately has also taken a few pieces. She thought perhaps some of the gentlemen would take them upstairs for her."

"Out with Colonel Jack, is she?" Alger asked.

"Yes, they are dining at the Clarendon, if you please."

"Oysters for Renie tonight!"

"I see you are familiar with the routine."

"Only the early part of the evening," he said, with a daring little smile.

"I shouldn't think the colonel is up to any strenuous postprandial pranks. He is scarcely able to walk without help."

"After a dozen oysters, there is no saying.

64

Which pieces are Renie's? I shall ask Butler to help me take them up. We can leave them outside her door."

"I have a key. She said I might unlock her door."

Butler came back down for another chair, and Alger collared him to help with Miss Whately's selections. I went up with them to unlock her door.

"There is a lamp and tinderbox just there on the sofa table," Alger said.

I made note of his familiarity with the room, but said nothing. I rooted in the dim light from the hall and found the lamp and tinderbox. Renie's parlor was a completely different affair from Mrs. Clarke's. It was bright and lively, but incredibly messy. The walls held playbills from a decade ago, with Irene Whately's name prominently displayed. The theaters were not Drury Lane or Covent Garden, but small provincial theaters whose names I did not recognize.

Various bright shawls, bonnets, and gloves littered the sofa. A decanter of wine and some used glasses sat on the sofa table. I thought she must have been reading there, but there was no novel or even magazines anywhere to be seen. I remembered her "leaving her specs behind," and wondered if it was possible she was illiterate. It seemed odd there was not even a journal or letter in the place. A pair of slippers had been kicked off in the middle of the floor. I moved them aside, so the gentlemen would not trip over them.

"Just leave the dresser there. Miss Whately can put it where she wants it later," I said.

We returned belowstairs, Butler to get Miss Whately's chairs, Alger to get his desk. To speed up the removal, I carried up one of Mr. Alger's chairs, Miss Thackery the other. I was eager to see how Alger had done up his parlor. The other rooms had reflected their owners somewhat. Perhaps I could find a clue to Mr. Algler in his arrangement.

I was disappointed. The room had a sterile look. It was tidy, but very little had been added to the basic minimum my aunt had supplied. There were some books in good leather-and-gilt bindings, a welter of folders and papers on the sofa table, and a few elegant bits and pieces that stood out in contrast to the rest. The wine decanter and glasses, sitting on a silver tray, had the prismatic sparkle of crystal. On a side table there was a chess set, with a board done in squares of dark and light marble. Handsome carved marble pieces were scattered over the board, indicating a game in progress. A crystal ink pot and some desk accessories were also there.

"You see why I required the desk," Alger said. He had come up behind me. "Sharkey is my usual chess partner. I fear I cannot match him for skill. Did he settle his account, by the by?"

"Yes," I said, and blushed to remember how I had been talked into taking that valuable watch.

"The ruby ring?" he asked, with a brow lifted in concern.

"Ruby? He said it was garnet."

"Looked like a ruby to me. I would not advise you to accept anything but cash from him, Miss Irving. One dislikes to speak ill of a man behind his back, but I once bought a watch from him and lived to regret it."

"What happened?" I asked in alarm.

"A constable came and relieved me of it. I narrowly avoided incarceration myself. 'Receiving stolen goods,' I believe was the charge. I managed to convince them of my innocence."

"You mean he is a *thief?* He said he bought up bankrupt shops and households."

"He does that, too, upon occasion." My distress must have been evident, for he said. "Miss Irving! You haven't... ?"

"A watch," I said, and drew it from my pocket. Now that I knew why he had asked for secrecy, I did not feel guilty about revealing the transaction. "I got it for Miss Thackery's birthday. She lost her watch. Oh, dear, I must give it back to him at once. I wish you had warned me, Mr. Alger."

"It was my intention to warn Sharkey off from pulling this stunt on you. I even—" He stopped and just frowned.

"You gave him money to pay his rent! You did, confess it, Mr. Alger. I saw you giving him money."

"You don't miss much! It was a loan. He always repays his loans, one way or another."

"That was very kind of you, but I fear kindness is wasted on Mr. Sharkey. I shall ask him to leave."

"Oh, I would not be too hasty, Miss Irving," he said, with an ingratiating smile. "Heaven knows who you would find to replace him. He is having a difficult time making ends meet at the moment, but he always pays eventually. He supports his widowed mother, you see, and four younger sisters."

"That is kind of him to be sure, but I shall give back his watch all the same."

We went to Mr. Sharkey's room and knocked on his door. There was no answer. We ran straight downstairs, only to find that Mr. Sharkey had left. "I shall give it back to him first thing tomorrow," I said, "and in the meanwhile, I shall hide it in a vase, in case the constable comes to search me."

"They are not allowed to search your house without a warrant," Mr. Alger said. I must have looked suspicious, because he felt obliged to explain his knowledge of this fact. "You will not be acquainted with Sharkey for long without learning the rudiments of your legal rights," he said, with a smile. "It is quite an experience, learning how the other half lives, is it not?"

" 'Experience' is one word for it."

"You must not let yourself become so upset over these trifles, Miss Irving."

"Trifles! I am a receiver of stolen goods! I might be locked in the roundhouse before morning."

"Perhaps he came by the watch legitimately. And in the worst case, I can recommend an excellent lawyer. He will get you off with a couple of years. I am *joking*, Miss Irving! I think you require a glass of wine."

He poured a glass of wine and took one himself. I could see Mr. Alger was upset over something. He was silent, and wore a puzzled frown as he sipped his wine. But before he left, he made the effort to be more sociable.

"You have not forgotten we are to visit Somerset House tomorrow?"

"No, I have asked Miss Thackery to join us. I hope you don't mind."

"I should have told you to invite her. That was remiss of me."

It was the gentlemanly thing to say, yet I was a little disappointed that *he* was not disappointed at her coming. He soon went upstairs, and Miss Thackery joined me. She had made tea and brought a tray to the saloon. We discussed how we would rearrange the room tomorrow, now that we were rid of most of the excess lumber. I would ask Mullard to chop up the few remaining pieces for firewood. Miss Whately could have one of the spare carpets, and no doubt one of the other tenants would be happy to take the other off our hands.

Miss Thackery noticed the wine decanter was empty and asked Mrs. Scudpole to bring a fresh bottle. She brought it and said grimly, "This is the last bottle in the house."

"Surely my aunt had a wine cellar? Did you look in the cellar?"

"I got this one from the cellar. The last one." She gave us a dirty look and left.

I did not mention the watch to Miss Thackery. She would want to turn Sharkey off at once, but I kept thinking of the poor man—having to support himself and his mother and four sisters. Another tenant to feel sorry for.

Chapter Seven

It had been arranged that I would take over my aunt's bedchamber, while Miss Thackery slept in the room we had both used the night before. We retired early, which was a very good thing, for from one o'clock onward, we scarcely got a wink of sleep that night. At one o'clock, Miss Whately came home utterly foxed. The colonel was in a similar condition. We had determined earlier that the tenants each had their own key for the front door, but the job of inserting a key in the lock was beyond the combined talents of the pair of them. They banged on the door, frightening the life out of Miss Thackery and myself. When we tiptoed into the hallway, armed with a poker and a water jug respectively, the giggles and singing on the other side of the door told us what was going forth.

There they stood, leaning against each other for support, smiling like a pair of moonlings. Miss Whately's bonnet was knocked sadly askew, and her gown looked as if she had slept in it. The colonel's cravat hung around her neck. He looked excessively rakish with his cravat missing from his toilette.

"Oh Mizz Cummings, I've gone and forgot my key," Miss Whately said, and laughed uproariously. She held the key in her fingers, but it was a key from the colonel's ring that was wedged partway into the lock.

The colonel smiled blearily when the door opened. "You see I am in deshabille," he said, slurring the words. "This young miss took my cravat. She could talk a cow out of its heifer." He looked at his key—and at the open door. "Told you mine would work," he said to Miss Whately. "Always opens *my* door."

"I'm glad something about you works, Jack," Miss Whately replied, with a lecherous wink in my direction.

She stepped in; the colonel tried to follow. I let Miss Whately pass, but put my arm out to bar him from the door. "Good night, Colonel," I said firmly.

"Eh? Why, it is the shank of the evening. Renie has asked me up for a glass of wine."

"You have already had quite enough wine."

"I have not touched a drop! I have been drinking brandy."

He tried to barge past me, but his innate breeding prevented him from manhandling a lady. Soon he discovered something else to divert him. My dressing gown had come a bit loose as I worked to keep him out. He peered down it and said, "I say! That's a bit of all right!"

"Colonel Stone!" I exclaimed, clutching my gown about me.

"Don't mind him, dearie." Miss Whately smiled in a fatuous way and slid his cravat around my neck. "He talks a good game but there is no vice in Jack, is there, darling?"

"No, no. I am Simon Pure." He smiled, reaching to snatch my gown open.

I gave his hand a hard slap. "Go home, Colonel," I said severely, and closed the door. I set the lock and turned to Miss Whately.

"Jack likes that, you know," she said, nodding her head wisely. "A bit of slap and tickle is just up his alley."

"Can you get upstairs by yourself?" I asked.

"We'd best give her a hand or she will rouse the house," Miss Thackery said. As her flat was on the third floor—and it was fourpence to a groat she would not be able to get her key in her lock anyway—we assisted Miss Whately upstairs. She spoke loudly in her resonant voice all the while, as if she were pitching her lines to the farther row of the balcony.

"A lovely man, the colonel, Mizz Cummings. What a grand meal he bought me." She stumbled and nearly sent Miss Thackery tumbling downstairs. "Oh, you're not Mizz Cummings. You're Mizz That— Miss T."

When we finally got her up one flight, she burst into song at the top of her lungs. "My Jack's a Soldier," was the song, and she sang it lustily.

Mrs. Clarke's door opened a crack. "Oh, it is only Renie," she said, stifling a yawn, and closed her door again.

Almost at once, Mr. Alger's door opened. I was surprised to see he was still wearing his evening suit. I had thought he would have retired by one o'clock.

"Can I give you a hand, Miss Irving?" he asked, and came to assist us. "Shame on you, Renie," he scolded, but he scolded tolerantly. "What will Miss Irving think of you?"

"Oh, ho! Miss Irving ain't as nice as she's cracked herself up to be, Algie. She was rolling her eyes at my Jack. I saw you flaunting your bosom at him, Miss Irving," she said, shaking a finger at me. I gasped in dismay.

"I would like to have seen that," Mr. Alger said, grinning. Then he got a strong arm around Miss Whately and began urging her forth.

Miss Whately fell back in his arms. With her unfocused eyes gazing up at Mr. Alger, she crooned, " 'My Jack's a soldier; he's gone to war.' He's a grand man, is Jack," she added, not in song. "And you're not so bad yourself, Mr. Algie. You'll join me for a wee glass of wine when we get rid of *her*," she said, tossing her curls in my direction. "But you must not seduce me, naughty boy." So saying, she wrapped both her dimpled arms around his neck and attacked him.

Mr. Alger gave an appealing glance, and I went to his assistance. We finally got her in motion again. Miss Thackery and I took her arms; Mr. Alger put his weight behind her; we nudged her upstairs one step at a time, to the accompaniment of yelps and giggles and song. I unlocked her door, and we deposited her on the sofa.

"We should not leave her like this," Miss Thackery said. "We ought to get her into bed."

"Oh Miss T"—she smiled—"you are giving Algie ideas."

"She will have a crick in her neck by morning, rolled up on that little sofa," Miss Thackery said, with a *tsk*.

"She will have worse than a crick in her neck. Her head will feel like a thundercloud, but that is not our fault," I said. "Let us leave her. I am sorry we disturbed you, Mr. Alger, but I see you had not retired yet."

"Happy to help. I was just reading over some correspondence for Dolman," he replied. "I shall turn in now."

We left him at his door and went downstairs. It was not easy to recapture sleep after such a disturbing interlude. We discussed whether we should turn Miss Whately off, considering the disruption she caused our other tenants. By two o'clock I was beginning to doze off again. At five past two, there was an infernal pounding on the front door. Of course it roused Miss Thackery, too. She came to my door and said, "Who can that be?"

"Mr. Sharkey is the only one who went out. He must have forgotten his key. Pest of a man."

I put on my dressing gown, snatched up a lamp, and went to open the door, with Miss Thackery bringing up the rear. I unlocked the door, trying to decide whether to tackle Sharkey about the watch that night, or wait until Miss Thackery was not about. To my amazement, I found myself confronted by a tall, glowering Bow Street Officer. He shoved a piece of paper at me.

"I have a warrant to search the premises of Eric Sharkey for stolen goods," he said, and marched in.

I could see nothing for it but to go along with the law. "Third floor, flat 3B," I said, and he marched up the stairs. He was every bit as noisy as Miss Whately. You would think the police could show a little consideration for the innocent people who had to rise early for work in the morning. Miss Thackery and I did not follow him upstairs. In fact, Miss Thackery said it was no better than she expected of Sharkey and returned to her bed in disgust.

I waited on the landing and saw Mr. Alger go into the hallway to speak to the officer. Alger was still wearing his evening suit.

"May I see that warrant, Officer?" he asked in a haughty way. The officer handed over the warrant. Alger examined it. Apparently it was all signed and sealed properly.

"Is Sharkey at home?" the officer asked.

"No, I haven't seen him this evening. What is the charge?"

"The usual. Receiving stolen goods. Lady Pryor had a ruby ring, a string of pearls, and a watch snaffled by a footpad earlier this evening. Sounded like the sort of goods Sharkey handles."

"He has been out of town for a few days, Officer. I think you must be barking up the wrong tree this time."

"I'll have a look over the premises all the same. Might find something else." He continued up the next flight.

Alger followed the officer up to Sharkey's flat, while I stood, dumbfounded. It was not a total shock that Sharkey had come by the watch and ring dishonestly. My own suspicion was that he had actually stolen them himself, but apparently he was only the middleman, buying stolen goods and selling them to the unsuspecting at bargain prices. What upset me more was that Alger was lying to shield him. And what was most disturbing of all was that I was actually in possession of the stolen watch. What should I do? I knew perfectly well I should hand it over to the officer and tell him how I had come by it.

I was a receiver of stolen goods, but an innocent one. Surely I would not be arrested on my first offense. I thought of Sharkey's poor widowed mother and those four young sisters. What would they do if Sharkey was tossed in jail? And Alger might go right along with him, for having lied to the police. Really it was a very difficult decision to make. I had still not reached any conclusion when the officer came down from Sharkey's room some minutes later, empty-handed.

"No evidence there. You are sure Sharkey has been out of town?" the officer said to Alger.

Alger, lying in his teeth, replied, "Quite sure. He left two days ago—a drapery shop in Cranbrook was selling out. He expected to be back by tomorrow."

"I may drop by for a word with him. Good night, sir. Thank you for your help."

"Any time, Officer. Always glad to assist the law."

I darted into the saloon and hid while the officer left. I nipped out behind him and locked the door. When I turned around, I emitted a yelp of shock. Mr. Alger was standing at the foot of the stairs, watching me with a quiet, snakelike gaze. I knew instinctively he was wondering how much I had heard. There was a tense, assessing look on his face.

"The officer searched Sharkey's flat," he said. "He didn't find anything." His noncommittal speech was an attempt to learn what I knew.

"How could he, when I have Lady Pryor's watch hidden in a vase and he still has the ring in his pocket? Why did you lie for Sharkey?"

"Why did you?" he asked, with a challenging look.

"I didn't!"

"By omission, you did, Miss Irving," he replied, walking slowly toward me. "You could have given the officer the watch and told him where you got it."

"I wish I had! I feel as guilty as a murderer. But why did you tell that plumper, Mr. Alger? Was it because of Sharkey's family?"

Mr. Alger wore the strangest, quizzical expression, almost as if he did not know what I was talking about. Then he recovered and assumed a sympathetic pose. "I don't know what those poor girls would do if anything happened to him."

"I doubt very much if he even has a family. I shall report him first thing tomorrow morning."

"Don't be absurd," he said sharply. "Of course he has a family. Why would I lie about that?"

"I don't know—unless you are in on it with him," I said, and was sorry I had given voice to this new possibility. Really it seemed the likeliest way to account for that fine marble chess set in Alger's room.

Alger's face stiffened dangerously. He was within striking distance of me now, and I was suddenly very aware that I was alone in this part of the house with a strong man who could strangle the life out of me if he wanted to. And he looked as if he wanted to.

He batted his hand and said impatiently, "Don't act too rashly, Miss Irving. You are not familiar with how the law treats people in this part of London. Sharkey might very well pay with his life. It is true he accepted stolen goods; it was wrong of him if he knew they were stolen. Very likely he was unaware of it. In any case, Lady Pryor can well afford to lose those few trifles."

"Surely they would not hang him only for that."

"That would depend on how his crime was interpreted. The laws are made to protect the goods and chattels of the wealthy, privileged class."

"But it is not right for him to help thieves, Mr. Alger. Surely you are not condoning his behavior."

"Of course not, but if he is arrested his sisters will end up on the streets. That seems a hard fate for those innocent young girls. The truth is, I am trying to reform Sharkey. He makes occasional lapses, but with you to ride herd on him as well, I think we might make something of him. This is his first lapse in two months. Let us give him another chance. Surely a minister's daughter must have some compassion." Mr. Alger spoke sincerely, almost with passion.

I was at a loss. I did not want to be too hard on Sharkey; I certainly did not want to be the cause of young girls taking to the streets, yet I did not want to be conned by a pair of crooks, either.

I said, "If Mr. Sharkey will return the jewelry to Lady Pryor—anonymously—then I shall give him one more chance. But if anything like this occurs again, Mr. Alger, I shall report him—and you—to Bow Street. What would Lord Dolman say if he knew of this night's work? You would lose your position and jeopardize your whole future."

"As a matter of fact, Lord Dolman takes a lenient view of such matters. He is very active on behalf of the underprivileged classes. It was his suggestion that I try to reform Sharkey."

It was late, and I was tired and troubled. I

had never had such a difficult moral decision to make before. A man's life was in my hands, and as I thought of how easy my privileged life had been until now, I felt some sympathy for Sharkey. Like Mrs. Clarke, his life was no bed of roses. Perhaps he had more need of my sympathy than Lady Pryor.

"Will you make Sharkey return the stolen items and see that he does not do it again?"

"It was my intention. In fact, you may wrap up the watch and ring and post them to Lady Pryor—anonymously—yourself. Will that satisfy your scruples?"

"Yes, if you include the pearls. The officer mentioned pearls as well."

"I don't believe Sharkey has the pearls. He could only afford the smaller items."

"Well, he must return the watch and ring then."

He smiled a smile that was worth a little bending of the law. It reeked of approval and a warmth that went considerably beyond approval. "God bless you, Miss Irving. I knew I might count on you. What a wretched time you are having in London. We shall have to do something about that. Such generosity deserves a tangible reward. Do you like the theater?"

"You don't have to bribe me, Mr. Alger. We have made our bargain."

"It was not a bribe!"

"A reward, then."

"I am flattened that you see it in that light. I would consider the reward my own, if you would let me take you out."

"The only reward I want is that you not mention a word of this to Miss Thackery, or she

79

would think I had run mad. I don't know what Papa would say…"

"I shan't tell either of them. It will be our little secret. There is nothing like a shared secret to forward a friendship," he said, with a warm smile. I gave him a sour look.

He reached out and took my two hands in his. "Come now, let me see that rebel heart. You are no longer a child who must look to her papa for moral guidance." His dark eyes studied my face in the shadowy hallway. "You are a mature lady, and an extremely attractive one."

I heard echoes of Sharkey's conning speech in that compliment and twitched angrily away. "Don't add insult to injury by trying to butter me up, Mr. Alger. As you say, I am a mature lady, and too old a cat to be conned by a pup's flattery."

"Pup!" he exclaimed. "I am one and thirty."

"Then you are too old to carry on in this ramshackle way. For God's sake, why do you not move to Berkeley Square and pursue your career in good earnest?"

His lambent gaze remained fixedly on my face. Then he smiled and said, "But who would help you push your inebriated tenants upstairs of an evening, Miss Irving? As you are kind enough to imply I am a gentleman, I think you should be urging me to stay."

"I suggested you leave for your own good."

"We should not always put our own good first. You know it would be unfair to see poor Sharkey hung for dabbling a few trinkets. I shall stay, if you let me, and see he does not sin again."

"Very well," I said, and was, in fact, relieved

that he was to remain. "And now I shall go to bed. If anyone else knocks at that door, I shall put my head under the pillow and ignore it."

"You really require a butler. Could your groom not fill that position for the present?" he said.

"I daresay he could." It was an excellent idea. I would ask Mullard to move in from the groom's quarters over the stable—which meant Miss Thackery and I must double up again. "Good night, Mr. Alger."

"Good night, Miss Irving." He turned to leave, then turned back. "About the theater, it was not a bribe, ma'am. I would like to take you and Miss Thackery one evening."

I just nodded and watched him leave. I kept thinking of that elegant marble chess set in his room—and the crystal decanter and glasses. Was he in league with Sharkey, accepting these trifles in payment for his lying to the police, or was he what he claimed, a reformer? I felt I would be awake all night worrying, but toward dawn, I finally dozed off.

Chapter Eight

I spoke to Miss Thackery the next morning about moving Mullard into the house to act as butler during the evenings only. We really needed a man about the place. This would not interfere with his cleaning up of the yard and painting of the front door—and such other minor improvements as occurred to us. During my sleepless night, I had come to the conclusion that the only sensible course was to sell the house. I was not equipped to live in this squalid neighborhood, with thieves and prostitutes. Charity begins at home; there were plenty of unfortunate souls in Radstock on whom I could practice whatever compassion and charity I possessed.

Strangely it was Mullard who would not hear of sharing sleeping quarters with the ladies. He toured the downstairs and found a cubbyhole off the kitchen that he said would suit him down to the heels. It was another storage area, and even contained, under a litter of boxes and bags, a truckle bed. Mullard spent his morning building a bonfire to burn the accumulated debris of my aunt's long residence at Wild Street. She had been the sort of lady who saved every journal and letter, every worn-out sheet and towel and facecloth.

Miss Thackery was busy emptying my aunt's gowns from the clothespress to make room for her own, and I was in my room, writing up a list of things to be done before selling the house. I had adopted the list-making habit from my companion. Getting that front door scraped, painted, and a knocker installed loomed large in my mind. The state of that door would be enough to put off any potential buyer.

Mrs. Scudpole came to my door and said, "Mr. Alger just came in. He wants a word with you in the hall, Miss Irving."

I went to the hallway, but he was not there. I looked into the saloon and saw him walking swiftly toward the window. He seemed to be behaving in a stealthy manner, and I wondered if he was looking out the window to see if someone was following him—Bow Street, perhaps.

"Did you want to see me, Mr. Alger?" I called.

He looked startled, but came forward with a smile. "I hope I am not disturbing you."

"Not at all."

He looked all around, and when he was sure we were alone, he handed me the ruby ring. "You have the watch?" he asked.

"Yes, in that tall vase with the grapes painted on it."

He retrieved the watch and gave me Lady Pryor's address, on Half Moon Street. "I got her address from the directory at Whitehall," he explained. "I have finished my work for the day. I hope you have not changed your mind about going to Somerset House with me?"

"No, I should like to see something of London before leaving, as it is unlikely I shall ever return. I have decided to tidy the house a little and put it up for sale at once."

He gave a weary sigh. "I feared last night's activities would give you a disgust of the place. We very seldom have two such interruptions in one night."

"I cannot live in such a place as this. Mr. Alger. I am extremely sorry for Mr. Sharkey's sisters, and for Mrs. Clarke, but really! I shall try to find some respectable person to buy the house—someone who will operate it as my aunt did, so that the tenants are not inconvenienced."

He nodded. "You are quite right. This is no place for a lady. Of course you could hire a manager to run it for you. You would still be making a very good income on the investment, as we discussed yesterday."

"I would not be making much after paying a manager."

"You could find someone who would be happy to do it for the use of one of the flats. Not necessarily the ground floor you use yourself," he added enticingly. "You could rent that for a good sum."

This peculiar insistence on my keeping the house seemed suspicious, yet other than keeping his own flat, what had Mr. Alger to gain by it?

"I really do not understand you, Mr. Alger. You could be living in luxury at Lord Dolman's mansion, and instead you stay here, where it is impossible to get a night's sleep for the drunken revelry and incursions by Bow Street."

"Oh, but I have a very charming landlady," he said, with a flirtatious smile.

But it was not the landlady he was interested in, or why had he suggested I hire a manager? I went to the desk and rooted in the drawer for a little box to hold the stolen ring and watch. An empty box that had once held headache powders served the purpose. I wrapped them up and addressed them for posting.

"I take it you have seen Sharkey, as you have got the ring," I said. "When did he get in? I did not hear him, and I was awake most of the night."

"I stopped at his door this morning. He was in; I did not ask him when he got home, but I warned him of Bow Street's visit. He asked me to give you this," he said, and handed me the month's rent.

I had a strong suspicion that money came out of Mr. Alger's own pocket. Where had Sharkey gotten it, unless he had robbed someone else?

"No, he has not been stealing again. He won

it at cards," he said, apparently reading my mind.

I wrote the receipt and handed it to Alger. Our business was done, but he did not leave.

"Have you had lunch?" he asked suddenly. "Why do you not get your bonnet and I shall take you out to lunch."

"We are very busy today. I really should not go to the exhibition, but I shall."

"It would not take long. We shall not be alone at the exhibition, Miss Irving."

There was some emphasis on that "alone" that suggested a personal interest. Mr. Alger was exceedingly handsome, and I was not immune to his charm, yet he was not a man to be trusted by any means. "No, really," I said, with a little blush of pleasure. "We have no need to be alone."

"Not an absolute need, perhaps, but a gentleman does like to be alone with a lady he—" He stopped and smiled. "I must learn to control this wayward tongue," he said. "You see what bad habits a fellow falls into, living among commoners."

"Yet you urge me to remain on here!"

"That might bring forth some very interesting results," he said, with another flirtatious grin. "But I am not trying to lead you astray. Far from it! Let us just go for a little drive. Get your bonnet. I shall show you Drury Lane Theatre. It is just around the corner."

"It will still be there this afternoon. You can show it to me then."

"Yes, and I can show it to Miss Thackery, too," he said, with a look of mock injury. "If it don't burn down again, that is. Have you seen it since it was rebuilt?"

"I have never seen it. This is my first trip to London."

"Good lord," he said, and stared as though I had just announced I had another head that I kept at home in a drawer. "I see it will be no problem to entertain you, Miss Irving."

"You need not feel constrained to entertain me, sir. I did not come to London for entertainment."

"I do not feel constrained! On the contrary. I look forward to it with great pleasure. But you still ain't going to get your bonnet and come with me now, are you?"

"No, Mr. Alger. I am not."

Our *à suivie* flirtation, for that was what our conversation amounted to, was interrupted by a scurry of footsteps in the hallway; Mrs. Thackery came in. "She's gone!" she said, with more satisfaction than annoyance.

Mr. Alger's eyes flew open, and he leapt to his feet. His face was snow white.

"All I said was that she must clean up that kitchen, for it is filthy, Cathy," Miss Thackery continued. She had not noticed Alger's overwrought reaction. "She flew into the boughs and told me she had enough to do cooking for three, without scrubbing floors. What is really bothering her is Mullard. She does not like having him sleeping in that little storeroom. As if he would be any menace to that old hag!"

Of course Miss Thackery's news was distressing, but I found myself studying Mr. Alger as the color seeped back into his cheeks and his body relaxed.

"Mrs. Scudpole has done a flit, has she?" he asked in a conversational tone.

"Who did you think Mrs. Thackery was referring to, Mr. Alger?" I asked. Who else could it be? Mrs. Clarke, or Miss Whately. There were no other women in the house. Oh, and Miss Lemon. Of the three, I felt it was only Mrs. Clarke who could possibly have caught his interest.

"I assumed it was Mrs. Scudpole. If I looked surprised, it is only that I was expecting to hear she had taken the silver with her. Yet another reason to make you want to leave."

"No, she did not," Miss Thackery said, "for I was right there, you know, and she could hardly rifle the silver chest under my very nose. What are we to do for a servant, Cathy?"

"We must be in touch with an employment agency and find a temporary maid who cooks, or a cook who will do a little cleaning."

"No one decent will ever come to Wild Street," Miss Thackery said, giving tongue to my own fear. "At least we shan't starve. I know how to cook a little, and between us we can make our beds and do the dusting."

"Honest work is hard to come by in this part of town," Mr. Alger said. "You will not have much trouble. I shall put the word out, if you like."

"A young girl would be best," Miss Thackery said, smiling in relief. "I can oversee her cooking. What we really need is a strong back and a good worker."

"Mrs. Freeman, just down the street, has a couple of girls who do odd jobs while awaiting their chance in the theater," Mr. Alger said. "Your aunt used to use them as occasional help for the spring cleaning and so on. Shall I speak to Mrs. Freeman now?"

I said, "That would be a help, if you don't mind."

Mr. Alger left at once. I noticed that his eyes turned to the window before leaving—and wondered if Bow Street was lurking about, on the qui vive for Sharkey. I strolled to the window, but no one was there.

"That was a stroke of luck," Miss Thackery said. "Very kind of Mr. Alger. He seems nice. What was he doing here, Cathy? Just a social visit?" she asked, her eyes shining with curiosity.

I disliked keeping so many secrets from my old friend. "I suppose you might call it that," I said vaguely.

She mistook my disturbed condition for embarrassment at being caught unattended with a beau. While she chatted on about Mrs. Scudpole's departure and the new girl, my mind wandered to more pressing problems. How was I to get the ring and watch to Mrs. Pryor? Miss Thackery would be with us on our afternoon outing. Like Mr. Alger, I rather wished she would not be. Perhaps I could have Mullard post the parcel while he was out for the paint and door knocker. At least Mr. Alger had been good to his word about returning the purloined ring.

Miss Thackery said she was going to make us a sandwich and tea, and while she did this, I took a dust cloth to the saloon. It had been impossible to clean it when it was so overcrowded, but now that it was clear of debris, I saw it was not an unhandsome room. The ceiling was lofty and the dimensions were generous. The double window gave good light, which unfortunately made the beggar's velvet decorating tables and lamps even more noticeable.

The furniture required beeswax and turpentine and a deal of elbow grease, so I just got a dust cloth and dusted the smaller items. There were two handsome china vases on a desk between the windows: the tall one decorated with grapes was the finer of the pair. The other was a shorter, bulbous one ornamented with peaches and apples. I lifted the latter and heard something rattle inside it. I peered in and saw a puddle of white beads of some sort. I tipped them out and held up a string of beautiful pearls. They glowed in the sunlight with a dull, iridescent sheen. The clasp was made of small diamonds. My gasp of delight hung on the still air. For a moment I thought my aunt had put them there and forgotten them. What a beautiful surprise!

Then I recalled the Bow Street Runner's list of items stolen from Lady Pryor—and I knew that what I held had not belonged to Aunt Thalassa. Sharkey had been standing by this desk last night. He had dropped the necklace in the vase for some reason. Perhaps it would be harder to sell than the less valuable ring and watch, and he did not want to leave it in his flat in case Bow Street called. My next thought was whether Sharkey had lied to Alger about not buying them, or had Alger lied to me?

I soon deduced the answer. Alger knew the pearls were there. He had been trying to recover them when I came upon him, hastening toward the vase. It was not the window he had been going to, but this vase. That was why he had been so insistent that we go out "alone."

He had asked me to fetch my bonnet two or three times. And while I went for the bonnet, he would have pocketed the necklace. He was definitely Sharkey's accomplice.

The pearls were large, and it was a long necklace. This would be worth ten times the value of the ring and watch. It had not been much sacrifice for Sharkey and Alger to return the smaller items to keep me silent. And to allow them to stay on at my house. That seemed very important to Mr. Alger at least. I took the necklace and hid it in my bedchamber, lest Sharkey or Alger come looking for it. But I would wrap it up with the other items for Mullard to mail to Lady Pryor—and I would give Alger a good Bear Garden jaw, too, for trying to con me.

Miss Thackery and I had our sandwiches and tea and the remains of a stale plum cake, and as we were rising from the table, Mr. Alger returned with a young girl whom he introduced as Mary Freeman.

She seemed a rough-and-ready sort of girl in her early teens. She had a wide smile and a tousle of red curls. Her dress of blue dimity was clean, and she carried a white apron in her hand.

"I do mostly general cleaning, miss," she said, "but I can do simple cooking. Gammon and eggs and roast a chicken. Ma says she'll supply you with bread and sweets. She makes a dandy cake or pie."

"I shall show you what needs to be done," Miss Thackery said. "You can begin by putting on that apron and clearing the table, Mary. The kitchen must be scrubbed down. I shall make dinner myself tonight."

"What about our trip to Somerset House, Miss Thackery?" I said.

"I forgot all about it. You go ahead, Cathy. I can go another time. I cannot live in this house, knowing that kitchen is so dirty."

When Mr. Alger turned a laughing eye on me, I felt obliged to object. "I shall stay and help," I said.

She insisted I go ahead, and as I wanted a private word with Mr. Alger, I allowed myself to be persuaded. It was obvious that Miss Thackery imagined I had found a beau. She would be sorely disappointed.

Before going upstairs to freshen his toilette, Mr. Alger said. "Have you seen Professor Vivaldi today, ladies?"

"He went out early," I replied. "I believe he goes to the British Museum to do research."

"I just wanted to check a few Latin quotations with him, for a speech Lord Dolman is giving in the House."

"Surely Lord Dolman knows Latin," I said, surprised.

"Just so. I explained myself poorly. I wanted to ask Vivaldi if he could give me a couple of pertinent quotes. Dolman recognizes Latin, but like myself, he cannot always put his hand on the right quotation. There is nothing like a sprinkling of Latin to impress the House."

He left then, and I found a larger box to contain the pearls and the other jewelry. I smuggled my parcel to Mullard for posting. Lady Pryor would definitely get back her pearls and ring and watch. I had managed to outwit Alger and Sharkey, and it gave me courage to face the coming confrontation.

Chapter Nine

I wore the new chipped straw bonnet I had bought for spring and my best blue pelisse, not to impress Mr. Alger but to cut a dash at the exhibition.

"Very fetching," Alger said, smiling approval at the bonnet as we went out the door.

He assisted me into the curricle, but before mounting the box himself, he said, "I have forgotten my handkerchief. I shan't be a moment. Pray excuse me."

"Mr. Alger! Do not leave me alone with your team!"

He was uncomfortable with the social lapse of leaving a lady waiting alone in the street, but I knew instinctively that mere discomfort did not cause his frustrated expression. While he stood undecided, I realized what he really had in mind.

"If it is the pearls you are after," I said, "they are no longer in the vase."

Alger gave me such a scowl I was half afraid to set out with him, but as it was broad daylight, I felt fairly safe.

He hopped up on the box and led the horses off before speaking. When he had recovered his temper he said, "You knew all along?"

"No, I found them after you went to get Mary Freeman."

"What did you do with them?"

"They are on their way to Lady Pryor, Mr. Alger, along with her ring and watch. And don't

92

think you are going to weasel your way out of this one. You knew perfectly well the pearls were there! You planned to keep them, and try to convince me of your innocence by returning the less valuable pieces. How much does Sharkey pay you? Do you take your cut in chess sets and crystal decanters, or does Sharkey work for you?"

His reply was a bark of annoyance: "Don't be ridiculous!"

"Don't you take me for a fool."

"Sharkey did tell me the pearls were in the vase," he admitted. "He dropped them there for safekeeping last night. Bow Street does occasionally visit his rooms. I had already gotten the ring from him, to return to Lady Pryor. I meant to return the pearls as well. I did not wish to further aggravate you by telling you they were in your flat."

"A likely story!"

"No, a demmed unlikely one, but truth is oftentimes stranger than fiction. I could come up with a more convincing tale if I were trying to con you."

"Yes, you are good at inventing tales!"

"I am trying to reform Sharkey."

"Where is the thief now?"

"He is doing a little job for me."

"Then you *are* in charge! Stop the carriage this instant."

"A purely legal job," he said, through gritted teeth.

"Hah! He would not know the meaning of the word, and neither would you. What kind of job? Sharkey cannot know anything of politics."

"His errand has nothing to do with politics. It has to do with a horse I am thinking of buying. Sharkey knows horseflesh. He is trying the animal out for me. A hunter. I have been invited to hunt with Dolman's pack."

I kept his reply in mind, not believing nor quite disbelieving, but just mulling it over. "You gave Sharkey the money to pay the rent?"

"I lent it to him. He always repays me—not in stolen objects," he added angrily. "Good God! You sound as though I were a common felon."

"People are judged by the company they keep, Mr. Alger."

"Then you had best be wary of seeing much of me, Miss Irving, n'est-ce pas?" he said satirically.

"You may be very sure that has occurred to me, sir," I replied.

In truth, his little flare-up of temper did more to convince me he was innocent than any amount of smiling and flirting. He *could* have been looking for the necklace to return to Lady Pryor. He did not seem upset that I had returned it. We had been driving at a good clip toward the respectable part of town during our argument. Neither of us spoke for a few blocks. Then he turned to me and smiled a smile that told me I must be on my guard with him, for he had more charm than was good for a lady.

"Let us not spoil our outing, Miss Irving. I have been looking forward to it all day. As you plan to leave soon, we shall not have many opportunities to know each other. Somerset House has an interesting history, and a good location, right on the Thames. It was begun by Somerset in the sixteen hundreds, but he was beheaded before it was finished. The queens of Charles the first and second lived there. It was only at the end of the last century that it was put to public use." He continued on with other details of the house's history and architecture.

A gathering of carriages alerted me as we drew near the spot, and soon we had arrived. Alger found a linkboy to hold the rig for him while we took a look at the outside of the building. It was done in the Palladian style, with the long front facing the water. The Thames lapped gently at the shore. The cooling breeze was welcome on a warm day. Pleasure boats and some tugs were plying the waters.

Inside, the paintings were hung densely on the walls, one above the other, cheek by jowl, right up to the ceiling. Truth to tell, there was not one among them that excited my deep admiration. It was a landscape exhibition that was on display. I find nature so beautiful, and so easily accessible to be admired, that pictures of it seem superfluous. I had been hoping for a portrait exhibition, to see pictures of famous Londoners.

What I found more interesting than the art was the onlookers. I gazed in disbelief at the elegant toilettes London ladies wore on a simple afternoon outing. There were bonnets bearing whole gardens of silk flowers, complete with stuffed birds. My new chipped straw paled to insignificance, and my pelisse was the wrong color and material, too. All the ladies were wearing mantles of twisted sarcenet, green to compliment their flower bonnets. Mine was a blue worsted.

I was introduced to a few people. A Lady

MacIntyre and her daughter accosted Alger—
and gave me, my bonnet, and blue pelisse a
closer examination than they gave the artworks.

"Not one of the Season's better exhibitions,"
Lady MacIntyre complained. "One can see why
the crowd is so small."

It seemed like a goodish crowd to me. Looking
over the throng, I said, "Do you not think it
well attended, Lady MacIntyre? There must be
over a hundred people here."

"Oh, my dear, when you can count the viewers, the thing is a colossal failure." She laughed.
"When Reynolds and even Romney were alive,
the crowds were lined up for blocks. This is
not even a crowd, let alone a squeeze. Come
along, Samantha. We shall go to Hyde Park.
There is no one here. Shall we see you at Lady
Bonham's rout this evening, Algie?"

"If time permits, ma'am."

"You are not accustomed to working for a
living, eh? Tell Dolman I was asking for him."

Lady MacIntyre nudged her butter-toothed
daughter forward to make a curtsy, then hauled
her away."

"Now the crowd is down to ninety-eight. A
definite flop," Alger said.

"I suppose you think I am a flat, thinking a
hundred is a crowd."

"Don't put words in my mouth, then throw
them back in my face. I do not think you a flat;
provincial, perhaps," he added, with a reckless
smile, and raised his hands as if to ward off a
blow.

"A Bath Miss, and proud of it, sir."

"Now you are giving yourself airs. A Radstock

Miss, I would say. Do they have as many as a hundred people in Radstock, or do the thundering herd of a hundred come from Bath for exhibitions?"

"It is quality that counts, not quantity. At least they go to look at the pictures, not gawk at the other viewers."

"I have not noticed you paying much attention to the pictures."

"That is because the pictures are so inferior. We have better exhibitions at Radstock." I made a point to examine the pictures for a moment after that jibe.

A moment later a pair of bucks came pelting down the stairs from the upper gallery and spotted Mr. Alger. They came forward, running their eyes over me in a blatantly assessing manner. They reminded me of Mr Cruikshank's caricatures of young bucks. One was tall and slender; the other shorter and stouter. Both looked like fops.

"This is a sad excuse for an exhibition," the shorter one scoffed. "Trees and barns, and not a pretty woman in the lot."

"Indeed it is. We are about to leave," Alger replied. "Nice meeting you, gentlemen."

"Hold on, Algie! Why don't you introduce us to the lady?"

Alger introduced the short one as Sir Giles somebody and the tall one as Mr. Soames. "I have not seen you before, Miss Irving," Sir Giles said. "Algie has been keeping you to himself, sly dog."

"We were about to leave," Alger said at once, and put his hand on my elbow to lead me out.

97

"Can you not wait a moment?" the one called Soames said, with a sly look. "Lord Evans is joining us."

For some reason, the name Evans rattled Alger. "No, we really must be going," he said.

We left, while a trail of laughter followed us. "Selfish, I call it!" Sir Giles called. "All your hard work is going to your head, Algie. Don't worry, Evans won't tell Lord Dolman you are taking an unscheduled holiday."

We left at such a lively gait that I was short of breath by the time we reached the carriage.

"Tell me, Mr. Alger, why are we running? Are you avoiding work, and afraid your patron will discover it? If that is the case—"

"Of course not!"

"Then I can only assume you are ashamed to introduce me to your friends. Had I known green mantles were de rigueur, I would either have obtained one or remained at home."

"Green mantles? What the devil are you talking about?"

"You must have noticed, all the ladies wore them."

"No, *I* was busy looking at the pictures," he riposted.

"If it is not my pelisse, and you are not due at work, then what—? You owe them money!" I exclaimed.

Alger gazed at me in disbelief, then a small smile lifted his lips. "What a refreshing lack of vanity," he murmured. "Most ladies would have judged—correctly in this case—that I did not wish to share you with other gentlemen."

"But then other ladies, one assumes, are unaware of your doings with Mr. Sharkey. I daresay your eagerness to keep me to yourself recommends a rapid return to Wild Street. We are certainly not likely to be pestered by the ton there."

"You want to meet the ton," he said. "And I more or less promised I would enlarge your circle of acquaintances if you remained in London."

"You need not worry about that. I have definitely decided to sell the house and return to Radstock at the earliest possible date."

"Mrs. Hennessey will be happy to hear it," he taunted. "But before you go, I must try once more to tempt you. I would not want you to base your idea of London dos on that appalling exhibition." I waited hoping to hear a mention of Lady Bonham's rout or some such thing. "Are you free this evening?"

"After being out this afternoon, I cannot desert Miss Thackery again this evening," I replied, hoping he would not take me at my word.

"I hope Miss Thackery will join us at Covent Garden."

The name conjured up visions of London high life. It seemed a shame to leave without seeing something of the real London. Miss Thackery would enjoy it, too.

"I have tickets for a performance at Covent Garden. A revival of Sheridan's *The Rivals*. I think we can all do with a little comedy after recent events." He waited while I pretended to vacillate. "No bribe, no reward—just an evening at the theater."

"I daresay Miss Thackery would enjoy it. Very well. We shall go if she agrees."

I did not foresee any difficulty there. As it was still early, we went for a drive out the Chelsea Road before returning to Wild Street. We did not meet any more of Alger's friends. I still had a lingering notion that he had been embarrassed by my provincial toilette and determined to do better that evening.

Just one other point bothered me, and I inquired why all his friends called him Algie, when his name was Alger.

"It is a nickname, as people named Smith are often called Smitty, and as I have heard Miss Thackery call you Cathy. Your name, I collect, is Catherine?"

"Yes."

"The privilege of calling you so, of course, is limited to your friends," he said soberly, but with a laughing look in his eyes. "Would it be impertinent of me to call you Catherine? Not actually encroaching on familiarity, you see, but as a sort of bridge to friendship?"

He was looking at me as he spoke—and drove right over a clump of sod that had been dropped by a farm wagon. "Algie! Look out!" I exclaimed, without thinking. I also clutched at his arm, as the curricle had very high seats, with little in the way of protection.

"I shall take that as permission," he said.

"We hardly know each other well enough to be on a first-name basis," I said stiffly. I pulled my fingers away when I noticed I was still holding on to him.

"I see it as a question of which comes first— the chicken or the egg. Using a first name hastens intimacy along, and as you plan to leave soon, we must either become friends rapidly, or not at all. A friend is a precious thing to lose, Miss Catherine. Did you notice the clever way I phrased that—just a little encroaching, but with the 'Miss' to lend it a touch of propriety."

"You don't know the meaning of the word. Furthermore, Miss Catherine is completely inaccurate. I am not a younger sister."

"You are quite right. I should have omitted the 'Miss' entirely. That will teach me to try to straddle the fence."

I was in a good mood with the pending trip to Covent Garden and did not argue when he continued to call me Catherine, although I made a point to continue calling him Mr. Alger.

After a few miles he turned the curricle around and returned to Wild Street. Mr. Alger left as soon as he took me home. As his friends had been joshing him about skipping away from work, I felt he was probably going to Whitehall. Within an hour, a lovely corsage of orchids arrived for me.

"I look forward to the pleasure of your company this evening," it said. The card was initialed, not signed. In fact, the initials were illegible, but there was no doubt in my mind who had sent it. The footman who delivered it was a splendid-looking creature in green and gold livery. I assumed Alger had borrowed him from Lord Dolman.

Miss Thackery and I spent the latter part of the afternoon planning and arranging our toilettes. We had not come prepared for such high living, but with a few borrowings from Aunt Thal's wardrobe we felt we would not disgrace Mr. Alger. I found a veritable peacock of a silk shawl, all embroidered with flowers and sprinkled with sequins and with a long fringe to boot. Miss Thackery thought it had a slight aroma of the lightskirt, but we knew we were years out of fashion and decided it would do. It would lend the necessary touch of style to my pomona green gown. Miss Thackery was to arrange my curls high with a pair of my late aunt's pearl combs. Miss Thackery found an elegant ecru shawl that she felt enhanced her own dark gown.

I kept an ear out for Alger's return. When he came in at six-thirty, I went into the hallway to thank him for the corsage. He blinked in astonishment and looked completely bewildered.

"But I did not send you a corsage," he said, and seemed a little embarrassed that he had not. "For the theater, you know, I did not think it necessary."

"Who could have sent it?" I asked. "You are the only gentleman I know in London."

He frowned, but soon came up with the answer. "Sir Giles! I knew that scoundrel was rolling his eyes at you! You see now that I had reason for hustling you away from my friends. Do you have the card?"

I had tucked it into my receipt book and showed it to him. We puzzled over the initials a moment. "That last letter looks like an *s*," he said. "Not Sir Giles, but Harley Soames."

"Oh, the tall one," I said. He was also the more handsome.

"I see you have been assessing them as potential escorts!"

"A lady always does so, Mr. Alger."

He gave me a conning look from the corner

of his eyes. "I wonder how I stacked up? I am as tall as Soames. And considerably taller than Sir Giles. How the devil did he discover where you live? He must have followed us all the way out the Chelsea Road. I made sure no one would—" He came to a guilty stop.

"No one would see you squiring a provincial? You have been caught out in your sin, Mr. Alger. Your reputation is ruined."

"Kind of you to be concerned, but I have no reputation worth speaking of."

"I should let Mr. Soames know I will not be going out with him. The footman did not wait for a reply. He has very elegant servants, does he not? All that gold lace. Do you have his address?"

"Yes, but—footman? Soames doesn't have any footmen. He hires a set of rooms at Albany. He makes do with a factotum who serves as his butler and valet and general dogsbody."

"It must have been Sir Giles who sent the corsage."

"Ah, yes, the *short* Sir Giles." Mr. Alger shrugged. "It is demmed presumptuous of him to assume you will be at liberty. Let him come— and leave without you."

"It seems an ill-bred thing to do, but really I cannot think of any other course, as he did not even include his address. Although the orchids are very nice," I added forgivingly. "Two of them. Quite extravagant."

"You like orchids? I shall bear it in mind, Catherine."

He managed to put some accent on my name that lent it an air that went beyond familiarity to encroach on intimacy. Or perhaps it was his smile that did the trick. He used his nice smile, which looked warm and open.

When he came to call that evening, he carried a corsage of orchids—three orchids. Miss Thackery wore the smaller corsage. We were all dressed and just about to leave when the door knocker sounded. Alger opened the door, and there on the step stood old Colonel Stone.

His lined and serred cheeks folded into a smile. "You are all dressed and waiting. Splendid! I knew I might count on you. And you are wearing my corsage. Most obliging, Miss Irving. I have hired a private parlor at the Clarendon." And oysters, no doubt. His rheumy old eyes struggled for a glimpse of my bosom, using the corsage as an excuse.

"I am afraid I am busy this evening, Colonel," I said, trying to quell the laughter that wanted to bubble out.

"Eh? What do you mean?"

"Miss Irving is going out with me this evening, Colonel," Alger said firmly.

The colonel measured his competitor's broad shoulders and grumbled into his collar. "Is Renie here?" he asked.

She had heard the rumpus and came peering over the stair railing. "Colonel! Are we going out this evening? I swear you forgot to mention it to me. Lucky I am free. I turned down an invitation to dinner just a moment ago." I knew perfectly well she had not had any callers. "You really should let me know beforehand. You can wait for me up here. I shan't be long."

The colonel looked at the stairs and replied, "I shall await down here, Renie. Do hurry. I am famished."

It was a comical beginning to an evening that was to hold further excitement before I got back to Wild Street.

Chapter Ten

We were wafted to Covent Garden in the unaccustomed splendor of velvet squabs and silver appointments, with a crest on the carriage door to tantalize the hearts of less favored mortals. In other words, Mr. Alger borrowed Lord Dolman's rig for the evening. "Don't I wish Hennessey could see us now!" Miss Thackery said sotto voce to me.

I had thought the Theater Royal at Bath was grand, but it could not hold a candle to Covent Garden. Covent Garden had burned down a few years previously—and had been rebuilt as magnificently as a cathedral. The imposing marble facade gave way inside to more opulence. It was constructed on classical lines with porphyry columns, plaster statues, and plush sofas in the long gallery. The boxes were similarly grandiose. I felt like a queen when we were shown to our box on the grand tier.

Around and below us, a sea of turbans, feathers, jewels, fans, and opera glasses waved gently. We arrived early on purpose to ogle the audience. Mr. Alger was busy pointing out Lord and Lady Castlereagh, a royal duke or two, and other celebrities. With my embroidered shawl and my three orchids—and Mr. Alger—who made as fine an appearance as any of the gentlemen, I felt I was finally a part of fabled London. If this was how life could be, then I must revise my notion of running home to Radstock.

Mr. Alger saw I was ravished with delight. He leaned over and whispered, "I have asked for wine to be brought to our box during the first intermission. I expect a few friends will drop in. During the second, we shall go on the strut in the lobby."

"Splendid, Mr.... Algie," I said, and smiled to show my pleasure.

A hush fell over the audience. A man in formal clothes appeared onstage to announce the play, and at that precise moment, a page boy came into our box. I looked to see what other treat Alger had arranged.

"Here, this is Lord North's box," the page said, glaring at us as if we were a bunch of heathens. "Yez'll have to clear out."

"My good man!" Mr. Alger exclaimed, jumping to his feet. "There must be some mistake. I have tickets for this box." He handed them to the page boy, who condescended to glance at them.

"For last week, sir," he said. "Lord North is just on his way in with a party of six. Yez'll have to vacate the premises."

"That is impossible!" Alger exclaimed, snatching back the tickets. As he studied them, a frown grew on his face. "You are right. Ladies! There seems to be some misunderstanding." His face was as red as a rose when he turned to make his apologies to us. "There must be some box empty," he said to the page. "As you see, I am escorting two ladies."

"Ye'd ought to have checked your tickets then,

mister. Come along. I'll see if I can find yez a corner to squat."

As we were hustled out of our magnificent box, the commotion drew attention to us. It seemed half the audience turned to stare at our shame. We watched from the hallway as a party of six were shown in. One of the gentlemen actually nodded and smiled at Alger, having no notion we had been occupying his box.

There was a whispered colloquy between Alger and the page boy. Money exchanged hands. A moment later Alger turned to us and said, "There is an empty box. Not quite as good as the one we were just put out of, I fear. I do not know how to apologize, ladies."

"It is no matter," Miss Thackery said. She felt sorry for him in his moment of shame. I felt the same way myself. "We do not have to sit on the grand tier, with princes and dukes. It is not what we are accustomed to, I assure you."

The page boy took us to what must surely have been the worst box in the house. It was on the lowest level, rammed right against the wall. We got a draft on our backs and an angled view of part of the stage. The seats were not luxuriously padded; they were of hard wood, and crowded on top of one another.

"I will darken both of Sharkey's eyes and draw his cork when we get home," Alger growled. "I paid him three guineas for that ticket."

"Algie, you flat!" I exclaimed. "You cannot afford such extravagance. Good gracious, I hope you did not do that only to impress us."

"Not us—*you*." he said, his glance just slanting

off Miss Thackery to make sure she was not eavesdropping. I was touched at his effort and felt very badly for him. I determined on the spot that I would express myself delighted with the evening, no matter what further horrors it held.

The play, at least, was excellent. The wine ordered for our box at the first intermission no doubt went to Lord North's party. "I told the page boy to reroute it here," Algie said apologetically. We waited, but neither the wine nor any friends came. We sat alone in our dark little corner, watching the festivities in other boxes. Algie suggested we go out, but Miss Thackery did not like to think of the wine coming and our not being there to receive it.

"The play is marvelous," I said a couple of times, to try to cheer him up. "And the theater is lovely! I have never seen anything like it, Algie. We are enjoying ourselves very much. Truly we are."

In the darkness he squeezed my fingers. "You are very kind, Catherine, but we both know this expensive evening has been a disaster. The only pleasure will be finding a blunt instrument and lowering it with considerable force about Sharkey's head and shoulders when we get home."

"Perhaps it was an honest mistake on his part. Let us go into the lobby at the next intermission, as planned. Perhaps we shall meet your friends there."

We were all ready for a little exercise by the time the second intermission came around. I noticed Algie limited our exercise to one end of the lobby—and not the end where the grander members of the audience stood in clusters, talking animatedly about the performance. Later, he found us a seat on one of the plush benches and went to bring us wine. I saw him chatting to some of those members of the ton and wondered why he was so reluctant to let us meet them. We had been sitting all evening. I, for one, would have preferred to walk about and mingle.

When he returned with the wine, he came alone. If his aim was to isolate us, however, he was outwitted by one gentleman. A rather handsome man followed Algie with his eyes, and when Algie came toward us, the man followed. He was soon bowing and smiling.

"Lord Algernon," he said. "I don't believe I have the pleasure of your friends' acquaintance."

Miss Thackery's wineglass trembled in her hand, spilling a few drops on her good gown. We exchanged a startled look. *Lord Algernon*!

Algie ignored the strange salutation. "Ladies, allow me to present Lord Evans," he said. "Evans, may I present Miss Irving and her companion, Miss Thackery."

"Charmed," Lord Evans said, with a gracious bow. "I expect you are Lord Algernon's neighbors. From Suffolk, are you?"

"Wiltshire, actually," Miss Thackery replied. I was quite beyond speech. "Near Bath."

"Ah, that would explain how you met. Lady Dolman was at Bath last winter. How is your mama's gout, Lord Algernon?"

"Much improved, thank you," Algie said in wooden accents. "And how is Lady Evans?"

"Oh, Mama is enjoying her usual vapors and swoons. She has put herself in the hands of a new quack who does not believe in either purging or bloodletting. No doubt he will be the finish of her. He has put her on a foolish regime of walking and eating a deal of fruit and vegetables. The fellow ought to be committed."

A little crowd soon spotted Evans and Lord Algernon and came along to pay their respects. Some of them had seen us being unceremoniously ejected from our box and laughed or consoled, according to their natures. I hardly heard a word anyone said, except that more than one of them called Algie Lord Algernon, and the name Dolman recurred, in close proximity, to "your papa." Once the cat was out of the bag, Algie relaxed somewhat—and even appeared to enjoy my confusion. That laughing light was back in his eyes.

"I shall explain everything later," he said in a low voice.

"You may be very sure of that, sir!" I hissed back.

This was why he had been in such an almighty rush to escape Lord Evans at the exhibition. The others, Mrs. MacIntyre and her daughter, Sir Giles and Soames, were on a comfortable first-name basis. Algie he could explain away as a nickname, but Lord Evans was more formal; he used the mysterious title. Lord Algernon had not wanted us to know he was Lord Dolman's son. I could not fathom why, nor why he did not live at his papa's comfortable house on Berkeley Square. He did not appear to be estranged from his papa, for more than one of the crowd made some joking reference to Dolman keeping the son's nose to the grindstone.

It was a complete mystery, but I had to wait

until the play was over before getting any satisfaction, for the crowd hung on until the bell announced the last act of the play. I had not seen or read *The Rivals*, and have to this day very little idea of how Lydia Languish and Anthony Absolute sorted out their various misunderstandings, but the smiles at the play's end told me it was accomplished.

My mind was fully occupied with Lord Algernon's masquerade—and the cause for it. Why had he said he was his papa's secretary? Why had he claimed he possessed only a small competence? Every word he had uttered thus far was a lie. The curricle he had supposedly borrowed from Dolman, the closed carriage we drove that evening—none of it made any sense.

After the play, Algernon suggested dinner at the Pulteny Hotel, where many of the crested carriages were heading. I would like to have seen the place, but knew it would not give us any privacy to hear the tale I was on nettles to hear.

"If you are hungry, milord, Miss Thackery and I will make you a sandwich. I am more hungry for an explanation of your deception than for food," I said.

"It is just as well. No doubt the table I reserved will have been taken by someone else, as I asked Sharkey to make the reservation."

We drove directly home, but we did not bother with sandwiches. Over sherry and biscuits, we finally got a story out of him. Whether it was the truth we had no way of knowing; it sounded quite farfetched to me.

"The fact is," Lord Algernon said, "my papa has been displeased with me. Gambling debts, a life of dissipation. He cut me off without a sou. Said it would teach me a lesson to have to support myself. So I fooled him and offered to work for my daily bread. He feared some of my friends would give me a synecure and insisted I work for him—and still support myself on my very minimal earnings as his secretary."

"You said he wanted you to live at Berkeley Square," I reminded him.

"Yes, after a few months he did rescind his harsh terms to that extent, but by then I had made up my mind to show him I was not the wastrel he took me for. Our friends are all aware that I have been sent to Coventry and josh me about it. You must have noticed, Catherine, that several of the people we met teased me about my work."

"Yes, I did notice that, but why did you tell me you were Mr. Alger?"

"Pride, I suppose."

"You need not be ashamed of honest work just because you have a title, Lord Algernon!" Miss Thackery said at once.

"That was not my meaning, ma'am. I did not wish to tell you I was the black sheep of the family and hoped to pass for a worthy, striving gentleman of modest means. As to the others, I thought I would fit in better with the tenants if I ignored the title. You must own, a lord living in a couple of hired rooms in this neighborhood sounds improbable. They would not have believed it, nor would you, I daresay. My being Mr. Alger saved explanations. I meant no harm."

Miss Thackery nodded her comprehension of this speech. "Wise of you, milord. Sharkey would have robbed you blind, and as to Miss Whately..."

"It seems very strange to me," I said. "Could you not have reformed yourself without moving to Wild Street?"

"Perhaps, but Papa was quite angry at first. The salary he pays did not permit me to hire rooms at Albany, or any such address. He felt me good for nothing and wanted to show me a lesson. Later, after we both got over our fits of temper, I still wanted to show him one."

"Well, you have showed him his lesson now and ought to return home. This is no place for a gentleman," I said severely.

"Oh, you shan't be rid of me that easily, Catherine. I shall stay out my year. I find Wild Street quite congenial... now." He gazed into my eyes as he emphasized that last word, implying that I was the cause of its new congeniality.

Miss Thackery suddenly decided we all needed some solid food—and used its preparation as an excuse to leave us alone. She thought she smelled romance in the air, but I discerned a fishier aroma.

"What about your dealings with Sharkey?" I asked. "Would Lord Dolman approve of you assisting a common felon?"

"He always has a soft heart for a reformer. He approves."

"You will never reform Eric Sharkey."

"Never say never. I reformed me," he said.

"Were you really that bad?" I asked reluctantly.

"I wasted a deal of time and money. I did not ruin innocent maidens, or cheat at cards

113

or kill anyone. You tell me how bad that makes me. Am I irreclaimable?" His smile was a challenge, and an invitation.

"I am not well enough acquainted with you to know."

He watched me a moment, then said, "My own feeling is that with the right lady to keep me on course, I could become an honorable member of society." He set aside his sherry and reached for my fingers.

I moved them away. "What is bothering you, Catherine? Is it the chess set, the crystal decanter? I like a game of chess. The set was a birthday present from Mama a few years ago. I did not feel I was breaking the terms of my bargain with Papa by bringing it with me. As to the crystal wine decanter and glasses—well, I can do without my valet and groom, and without a few of life's refinements, but I cannot and will not drink wine out of a cup. I bartered a pearl shirt stud for them at a pawn shop."

"You have an answer for everything," I snipped.

"Unlike you, who have not answered my question."

"You did not ask me a question."

"I implied one. What I meant was, are you interested in reforming a ne'er-do-well who is eager for reformation?"

"I believe Wild Street offers people in greater need of help than you, Lord Algernon."

"My friends call me Algie, Catherine."

"I only met you an hour ago, Lord Algernon. This sets our acquaintance back, does it not? You really must not use my Christian name on such short acquaintance."

"No, no! After all, *I* have known *you* for several days. You *are* still Miss Irving, are you not, from Radstock?"

"That is correct. I am Miss Irving, and I would appreciate it if you would call me so."

"Oh, no. I will not give up my hard-earned privilege. I am not totally reformed yet, you see." I believe he was about to revert to his abandoned ways, but unfortunately Miss Thackery came in with cold mutton and bread, and our privacy was over.

Miss Thackery subjected him to a discreet but thorough catechism of his family, his home, and other subjects that indicated she had shoved him under the microscope for examination as a potential husband. I listened sharply, but with an air of ennui to conceal my interest. We were just finishing our tea when the front door opened and someone came in. I noticed then that Algie had placed himself facing the hall, so that he had a view of anyone entering.

"That cannot be Miss Whately," I said. Footsteps were moving quickly up the stairs. There was no singing.

"Sharkey," Algie said, with a menacing grin. "Excuse me, ladies. I have a little business to discuss with Sharkey. Thank you for a lovely evening."

We insisted that the pleasure had been ours, and as Algie moved to the stairs with a meaningful stride, I said, "Algie, for goodness sake don't cause a commotion so late at night. Take him outside before you use that blunt instrument."

"You'll never hear him fall," he said, and ran upstairs.

I waited, listening, at the foot of the stairs when Miss Thackery took the tray to the kitchen. Not a sound came from above. Sharkey was on the third floor, however, and I feared any racket would disturb Mrs. Clarke and Jamie, whose rooms were below his. I went up to the second-floor landing to listen. From inside Algie's room, I heard the unmistakable sound of low laughter. Far from doing battle, Algie and Sharkey were enjoying a good chuckle. Then Algie spoke, but in no angry way. He seemed to be asking a question. His actual words were indistinguishable.

Sharkey had a loud, carrying voice. His reply was perfectly audible. "I followed her home all right. He didn't go near her. I think you're wrong about him, Algie. He don't seem to be interested in the girl."

Algie murmured something in reply. Sharkey said, "Don't worry, I'll keep an eye on her. But you'll have to take over yourself tomorrow night. Unless you want me to put off going to Stop Hole Abbey...?"

"No, no!" Algernon's objection was loud enough to be heard.

I tiptoed quietly back downstairs and went to my bedchamber. Stop Hole Abbey is a criminal haunt where stolen goods are traded. But Lord Algernon, the great reformer, not only refrained from discouraging Sharkey, he appeared to be the one encouraging him. In fact, as Sharkey asked his opinion, the only logical conclusion was that Sharkey was going at Algernon's request. Algernon was dealing in stolen goods. What would his papa say, and do, when he found out?

The story Algernon had told about his father suddenly seemed incredible. No rich and noble father would make his son live in such penury that he was forced to take rooms on Wild Street. Algernon was here because he wanted to work hand in glove with the detestable Eric Sharkey—for a share of the criminal profits. Algernon was a criminal.

I saved the most personal sin for the last. On top of his criminal activities, Algernon was so besotted with some girl that he had Sharkey following her, to see whom she met. Probably some proud beauty who was aware of Algernon's criminal streak. The only reason Algernon was trying to butter me up was because he liked the convenience of having a biddable landlady. If I had known all this last night, for instance, I would have turned him and Sharkey over to Bow Street.

It was too late now; the evidence was gone—but at least Lady Pryor had her pearls and ring and watch back. I had outwitted them that time. And I would outwit them again. Sharkey was off to Stop Hole Abbey tomorrow night. Very likely he would return with some other stolen goods. I would keep a watch on the front door, and if he went to Algernon—with his pockets bulging—I would send for Bow Street.

It was much later, just as I was dozing off, that I remembered Algernon had not upbraided Sharkey for giving us outdated tickets for Covent Garden. It had not bothered him a whit that we suffered the disgrace of being put out of our box. I renewed my resolution to sell the house and return to Radstock as soon as possible.

Chapter Eleven

I was up early the next morning. Before breakfast, I went to the kitchen and spoke to Mullard
about scraping and painting the front door. He
was enjoying a hearty breakfast of gammon and
eggs with Mary Freeman. Mary had worked
wonders on the kitchen. Its surfaces were all too
old and faded to gleam, but they were clean, and
Mary wore a clean apron and cap. It lifted my
spirits to see things being put to order, and to
smell the tantalizing whiff of coffee in the air.

I took a cup of coffee to the dining room to
await breakfast. I was just looking about for
the journals to discover an estate agent when
Mrs. Clarke's head peeked in the door. She
looked pale and tired, and her work clothes were
modest in the extreme, but neither a plain gray
round bonnet nor the air of fatigue could dim
her natural beauty. I said good morning and
inquired for Jamie's health.

"Good morning, Miss Irving," she said.
"Jamie is fine. He is teething and was awake
in the night, but he will be all right. I wonder
if I could ask a wee favor of you. I am expecting a parcel from my aunt today. She is sending some of her old baby clothes for Jamie.
Would you mind holding it for me? I'll pick it
up after work. Or you can just ask Miss Lemon
to take it up if it is in your way."

"I would be happy to, Mrs. Clarke."

"Thank you. I must dash. Mam'selle Lalonde
gets that cross if I am late."

I heard her speaking to Sharkey in the hall as she left. Such was Mrs. Clarke's youth and beauty that she nudged even Sharkey into civility.

"I am going your way, Mrs. Clarke," he said. "I'll walk along with you, if you don't mind."

"I will be happy for your escort, for they are tearing down that old building on the corner on my way to work... and some of the fellows shout and leer as I pass by."

"We'll see about that!" Sharkey said in a blustering way.

"Mr. Butler usually accompanies me, but he—" The door closed, cutting off her speech.

I remembered seeing Miss Thackery reading the *Observer* in the saloon yesterday and went to fetch it. As I was returning to the dining room, Lord Algernon came downstairs.

"Good morning, Catherine," he said, with a smile.

"Good morning, Lord Algernon," I said coolly. "Did you ring a peel over Sharkey last night? I must compliment you on your discretion. I did not hear any falling body."

"We have worked out a compromise. He gave me tickets—properly dated—for Drury Lane for tomorrow evening to make up for last night's catastrophe. I hope you and Miss Thackery will be my guests."

"Very kind, but we prefer to know what we are getting into when we go out with a gentleman."

"Cut to the quick!" he said, with an exaggerated grimace. "You will never let me forget that, will you? But as I said, these tickets are properly dated."

119

"I am sure the tickets are fine. Perhaps the colonel could spare Miss Whately to accompany you. I shall be busy making the house ready to show to potential buyers. I am just looking for an estate agent to call on this morning."

An expression more of hurt than anger creased his handsome brow. "What is the matter, Catherine?" he asked softly.

"I have come down with a bad case of reality, Lord Algernon. A pity you could not do likewise."

"What is that supposed to mean?"

"A clever scoundrel like you should be able to figure it out."

I left him standing in confusion with his hand on the banister post while I strode back to the dining room. I should not have let him know I was so angry. It might urge him to caution—and make it more difficult to catch him and Sharkey with their loot. I would be more conciliating the next time I met him, but I would not go out with him again.

I circled the names of a couple of estate agents within walking distance of Wild Street, according to a map of London Aunt Thalassa had in her desk. The only other item of interest that occurred that morning was a reply from Papa, positively urging me to remain on as long as necessary to get the house in shape for selling or renting. I sensed the fine hand of Mrs. Hennessey in his letter. It would suit her very well to have Miss Thackery and myself out of the way, to give her a clear field with Papa.

Later in the morning Mullard began scraping the front door. He used some sort of foul-smelling chemical to soften the paint. The reek

120

of it invaded the house, causing Miss Whately to come down and complain. At eleven-thirty in the morning, she had not yet put on a dress, but wore a garish flowered dressing gown.

"It's enough to give you a headache, Miss Irving. It can't be good for a body."

"He is nearly finished. I shan't keep you, Miss Whately, as I see you are just making your toilette."

"Oh, lud, I'm sick to death of all my clothes. If I have to put on that yellow gown again I'll wretch. Which reminds me, what are you doing with the old malkin's gowns, Miss Irving, if you don't mind my asking? What I was thinking—We're about the same size, me and Mrs. Cummings, except around the waist, and she had some dandy things. I couldn't begin to pay you what they're worth, but old Jack would be good for a couple of quid. He likes me to dress fancy."

"You are welcome to take a look, Miss Whately. There will be no charge," I added.

This being the case, Miss Whately, whom I was immediately urged to call "Renie," found much to her liking, even including colored silk hose with ladders and some antiquated shoes with gaudy silver buckles and other dramatic ornaments.

"You might ask Mrs. Clarke if she wants what's left," she said when she had her arms full to overflowing. "She's that handy with a needle, ain't she? You ought to see the neat mend she made in Mr. Alger's jacket sleeve. He ripped it when he was helping her put up Jamie's crib. Of course it stands to reason, her being a modiste and all. She'd be glad of a little extra work

121

if you need anything in the way of mending or sewing, Miss Irving. She makes all Alger's hand-kerchiefs and that."

It was thoughtful of Algernon to help the widow out in this way. I was glad there was at least a small streak of generosity in him. "That might be convenient. I shall see if we need anything. I expect Mr. Butler also gives her a little work."

"Yes, and even old Vivaldi. He has an eye on her, if you want my honest opinion. I've caught him more than once loitering round her door. Old enough to be her pa, the old hound. Of course he's no real competition for Mr. Alger."

"Surely it is Mr. Butler who has the inner track!"

"Don't you believe it," Renie said, and laughed. "He hadn't a look-in once she caught Alger's eye. Well, stands to reason, a swell like Mr. Alger. He's ever so fond of Mrs. Clarke. Takes her personal in his carriage when she has to go out of an evening. Says she's going to visit some friends of her late husband's. Straight to the nearest country inn, says I. Oh, that Alger is the one, ain't he? I wouldn't mind leaving my slippers under his bed—in a manner of speaking," she added, when I stared at her with my mouth open.

It was not her latest vulgarism that caused my jaw to drop, however, but the news that Algernon was seducing that nice Mrs. Clarke. I was furious, but I tried to conceal my rampant interest in this subject, while still extracting anything she might have to tell. "Would you like some coffee, Renie?" I suggested.

"I don't mind if I do, dear. I just ran out.

122

My last cup was so weak I had to help it out of the pot."

We went to the saloon, and I rang for Mary to bring coffee.

Renie said, "You've got this rat's nest fixed up ever so nice, Miss Irving. Who'd have thought it could look so swell."

"Yes, the proportions are rather nice, and the fireplace, too. Has Mr. Alger been seeing Mrs. Clarke for very long?"

"Ever since the day he moved in. He no sooner clamped his eyes on her than he was making up to her. In her room for an hour that very night, and Miss Lemon hadn't moved in yet, either," she said, nodding her head sagaciously. "In fact, it's him as found Miss Lemon, and it wouldn't come as a shock to me if he paid her wages as well. I mean to say, she's only got her man's half pension, hasn't she? How does she afford a full-time woman?"

"But she works as well."

"Oh, yes, but she once let out to me that she puts every penny of that aside for Jamie's education, if you please. And it's true, too, for I got a look at her bankbook."

I was strongly inclined to ask how she had achieved this, but thought it better not to know.

With her coffee cup in her hand, Renie became even more expansive. "Mr. Butler don't like it," she said, eyeing the sherry decanter.

I disliked to encourage her drinking and ignored the look.

"I've heard him jawing at Mrs. Clarke when she goes out with Alger," she continued. " 'You don't understand, Mr. Butler,' she says. 'Mr. Alger is just a friend.' Hah, with friends like that she don't need a banker. Comes home pink with pleasure when she goes out with Alger, and usually sporting some little extra the next day, I've noticed. That little chest in her parlor that she calls a chiffonier—whatever that may be—she got that after her first night with Alger. And the watch came after their second outing. Mind you, I'm not complaining. More power to her. Old Jack has been promising me a watch forever. I'll get it out of him one of these days."

Renie eventually finished her coffee and took her plunder upstairs. I sat on alone, thinking. Mrs. Clarke was certainly pretty. I already suspected Lord Algernon had an eye for the ladies. He was having Sharkey follow one, and he had been making up to me in a very practiced way. What surprised me considerably more was that the widow was open to his advances. I had not thought she cared for anything but Jamie. Was she doing it for her child, to make it possible to put money away for his future? That might help excuse her, but it was no excuse for Algernon. And for this, he was indulging in a life of crime, breaking the law and his father's heart, to say nothing of making me feel guilty for not helping the needy.

Miss Thackery came in from the backyard, where she had been battling with the garden, and told me Mullard was preparing to paint the door and did I want to check the color of the paint before he applied it.

It was a deep green, just as I had requested. Mullard had also bought a handsome brass lion's head door knocker that would lend us a touch of elegance—and no doubt make the one decent feature of the house emphasize the dilapidation of the rest. But at least my hands would not feel soiled every time I came in or went out.

Mrs. Clarke's parcel arrived while we were still admiring the knocker. I signed for it and took it upstairs. Miss Lemon came to the door, holding Jamie in her arms.

"He's teething, poor thing," she said. "Would you mind just putting the parcel on the sofa, Miss Irving?"

I was happy for another excuse into the apartment. My vulgar curiosity wanted a look at the chiffonier, Algie's first gift to the widow. It was an elegant piece with china ornaments on top and drawers beneath. Its newness was at odds with the rest of the room. Sitting on the end of the sofa was a familiar-looking man's waistcoat of yellow-and-maroon stripes. Miss Lemon noticed where I was looking and blushed.

"That looks bad, does it not!" she said, and laughed. "Mrs. Clarke is just tightening the buttons on it for Mr. Alger. She does a bit of sewing at home to help make ends meet."

"It is difficult for a young widow with a child," I said, quelling down my annoyance.

"Ah, but Jamie makes it all worth while for her. She fairly dotes on him."

Jamie began whining in discomfort. His little cheeks were bright red. "Does he have a fever?" I asked.

"He is a little warm, but it is the teeth coming in that causes it. I should give him his coral. Now where did I put it?" She looked around helplessly.

"Can I help?"

"Thank you. It must be in the bedroom, I believe. Would you mind seeing if it is in his crib, Miss Irving?" She pointed to an open door.

I went into the bedroom. It was Mrs. Clarke's room, with the child's spool crib in the corner. The modest decor was all arranged to suit the child. No fancy chiffoniers here, nor any toilet table with lavish accessories. The chest I had given her had been painted blue. There were toys on the matching set of shelves, and some pictures of animals hanging on the wall. Over her own bed, not a canopied bed but a simple lit, was a painting of an officer, presumably the late Lieutenant Clarke. He was handsome, with dark hair and dark eyes.

It did not look like the room of a kept woman, but of a poorish widow who put her child's welfare above everything. On the bedside table there was a book, facedown. I glanced to see what she was reading, thinking it would be the Bible, or a sentimental novel. It was a racy French novel entitled *Les Amours de Lise*. I snatched up the coral from the crib and took it to Miss Lemon.

She offered me tea, but I was on thorns to get away. What was Mrs. Clarke, who claimed not to understand French, doing with a French novel? It was open, facedown, to mark the place when she had stopped reading. Suddenly it did not seem so incredible that she was Lord Algernon's lover. I wished I had not gone upstairs and seen that bedroom. I knew Algernon was helping Sharkey to sell stolen goods, but to think he had seduced a poor widow was much worse.

Perhaps it was even Algernon who was reading

the racy French novel. Mrs. Clarke had definitely told me she did not understand French. There was no conceivable reason for her to hide this accomplishment. No, it had to be Algernon who was reading it, probably to her. He was sneaking into her apartment at night, when the house was quiet. That was why he had hired Miss Lemon. He needed a woman who would not object to the liaison. It was despicable— and it was going on beneath my own roof. I could not impose my morals on the world, but I could at least disassociate myself from the corruption.

It was becoming more obvious every moment that I must sell this house. London had lost all its allure; I might go to Bath, but I would not stay in London, where no one was what he or she seemed. London was too wicked for me.

Chapter Twelve

In the afternoon, Mullard drove Miss Thackery and myself to the estate agent's office. The man, a Mr. Simcoe, had ginger hair, cinnamon eyes, mustard teeth, and garlic breath. This spicy man was so eager for the commission that he returned to Wild Street with us in the carriage. For the next hour we heard the house denigrated in oblique terms. The location was "difficult," the condition of the premises "not optimum," the decor "far from ideal," and the income "hardly sufficient to excite interest."

He spoke so ill of it, I finally said, "Why Mr. Simcoe, you sound as if you were the purchaser, pointing out all its flaws. I expect my estate agent to concentrate on the building's good points when he is showing it to potential buyers."

He soon allowed that the brickwork did not appear to be perishing, and the chimney was intact. "You could subdivide the flats and make the income more interesting to a potential buyer," he suggested doubtfully. "Mind you there would be some expense entailed for carpentering, throwing up a few walls and doors, and so on."

"But what price do you suggest for the house as it now stands?" I asked. This was the great secret we had been trying to pry out of him for an hour, and he guarded it with his life.

"I can tell you what the house on the corner went for three years ago," he prevaricated. "Three thousand five hundred. Mind you it had been subdivided into more profitable flats."

"It is not as big or as nice as my house," I pointed out.

"Aye, but your buyer would not be purchasing to live in it himself. Such folks as live here don't have the blunt to buy, or they would be living elsewhere. What you get in this neighborhood is petty thieves and lightskirts, by and large, with a few honest modistes and clerks."

Sharkey, Renie, Mrs. Clarke and Mr. Butler. The description was so accurate that I could not argue. He had enumerated my tenants, only omitting Professor Vivaldi and Algernon. I remembered then, inconsequentially, that Renie had suggested even Vivaldi was interested in the modiste. Surely she was mistaken there.

"A price of five thousand was suggested to

me," I said, thinking of Algernon's evaluation of the premises.

"We might approach that estimation," Mr. Simcoe said doubtfully. " 'Twas three years ago the corner house sold, and as you said, yours is not quite so dilapidated. Shall we try her at five thousand and see if anyone nibbles? You can always come down to a more realistic price if you get any offer at all."

This did not sound very promising, but I said, "Very well."

The contract was under my nose so quickly I did not even see him extract it from his pocket. Before he left Wild Street, a sign was hammered with great difficulty into the rock-hard earth in front of the house. Before dinner, it had been yanked out and thrown away by the local ruffians. Mullard found it and hammered it into the ground again, and again it was rooted up within the hour. We finally put it in the saloon window, inside, where the local fellows would have to break the window to get at it, which was by no means out of the question.

Mr. Simcoe suggested I post a sign on the bulletin board notifying my tenants of my intention to sell as soon as possible, so that they might begin looking about for another flat. He seemed to take it for granted anyone foolish enough to purchase the place would immediately either raise the rates or make smaller flats.

The sign excited a deal of interest from the tenants, of course. Butler, whose dereliction in not escorting Mrs. Clarke past the leerers that morning was soon explained, was the first to come in. We learned he had been sent up to Camden Town by his employer on some official business. He came in at four. His first words were, "Does Mrs. Clarke know? I don't know what she will do, poor girl."

"The estate agent feels the buyer will continue to hire out flats, Mr. Butler," I told him.

"Yes, at some exorbitant price she cannot afford. I must run down to Mam'selle Lalonde's and tell Mrs. Clarke."

When Mrs. Clarke returned from work, she and Butler came to see me, both of them asking a hundred questions that I could not answer. I could not promise them the same rent when I did not yet have any offers.

"By Jove," Butler said, looking shyly at Mrs. Clarke, "if worst comes to worst, we may have to pitch in and share a flat, Mrs. Clarke. Heh-heh. Get married, I mean," he added, when she displayed a little interest in this notion.

"I don't know what Jamie would think of that," she said.

"Lad needs a papa, if you want my opinion," Butler said, though he said it in a joking way.

Still I found it curious that she did not squash the idea outright. She obviously knew there was no hope of an offer of marriage from Algernon. They ran upstairs together, talking animatedly.

"There is a match brewing there," Miss Thackery said.

I had not told her Renie's gossip about Algernon and Mrs. Clarke, but I had dropped a few snide comments about Algernon. She suspected no more than a lovers' quarrel and paid me little heed.

Sharkey returned a few moments after Mrs. Clarke. He must have seen the notice, but he did not come to speak to us.

The next arrival was Professor Vivaldi. He stopped at the saloon and said sadly, "I see you are selling the house, Miss Irving. I am very sorry to hear it. I daresay an old Benedict like myself can find a room somewhere, but I am worried about Mrs. Clarke. Has she mentioned where she will go?"

"Nothing is settled, Professor," I said. "We only put the sign up today."

"Poor girl," he replied, shaking his grizzled head. He was carrying a little brown bag. He opened it and showed us a set of tin soldiers in a wooden box. "I got these for Jamie's birthday," he said.

"Why Jamie's birthday is not for another three months, Professor," Miss Thackery told him.

"Is that so? I thought I heard her mention it was his birthday the other evening, when we were helping ourselves to your furnishings. That is my unfamiliarity with children speaking. I never had a son," he said. "I shall give her the toy soldiers all the same. I happened to find a set wearing the uniform of her husband's regiment. They will be a nice keepsake for Jamie, when he is a little older."

It is strange how you can be drawn into the lives of people with whom you share a roof. I found myself thinking the professor must have been eavesdropping when Mrs. Clarke told me that it was Jamie's nine-month birthday. She had not been speaking to him. This sharp interest tended to confirm Renie's farfetched notion that he was romantically interested in Mrs. Clarke. I felt, though, that it was the child who really interested him. He had looked rather pathetic when he'd said he'd never had a son.

131

"You will let me know if Mrs. Clarke finds another flat," he said. "I shall ask about among my friends and see if I can find her anything. Poor girl." He stuffed the box of soldiers back in the bag and went upstairs.

"He is lonesome," Miss Thackery said in a pensive way.

"He needs a wife, Miss Thackery. Perhaps you would care to apply for the position?" Miss Thackery always rises to the bait of this sort of teasing.

"Why not apply for a room in Bridewell while I am about it!" she retorted. "To be married to a poor man is a sort of prison. I know when I am well off, thank you. Now if he were a lord, that might be a different matter."

I pretended not to recognize this as a reference to Algernon. He was the last one to return that evening. He did not come to speak to us, either, but just hesitated a moment before running upstairs.

Mary Freeman roasted us a tasty chicken for dinner, and her mama was supplying us with bread and other baked goods. She had sent an apple tart that day. It was the best meal we had had since leaving Radstock.

After dinner, Miss Thackery went to the kitchen to help Mary, and I retired to the saloon to answer Papa's letter. He had not told me what should be done with Mullard and the carriage while we stayed in London. I feared he might be missing the carriage and asked if I should send Mullard home. While I was at this task, there was a great commotion on the stairs; going into the hall, I saw my tenants had descended en masse. I knew why they were there. They did not want me to sell the house.

Lord Algernon appeared to have been appointed spokesman for the group. He said, "We are very sorry to see you are selling the house, Miss Irving. We have all gotten together and discussed it. We wondered if you might reconsider if we voluntarily raised our own rent by ten percent. That would make your investment more profitable, and—"

"This was no trick to gouge my tenants, Mr. Alger," I said, using the name the tenants knew him by. "I only came to London to look the place over and put it up for sale. I am sorry it is an inconvenience to you all, but surely there must be plenty of flats to let in London."

There was a general murmur of disagreement. Someone mentioned that this location just suited them; another praised the cleanliness of the house, which made me wonder what conditions prevailed in other flats. Mrs. Clarke mentioned the generous size of the rooms, and Mr. Butler said something about the congeniality of the group. Neither thieves, prostitutes, nor lecherous lords were congenial to me, however, and I held my ground.

"In that case," Mr. Butler said to Mrs. Clarke, "let us hit the streets at once and begin scouting out other flats."

Most of the group had come down wearing their street clothes. Mrs. Clarke wore her bonnet; the gentlemen carried their curled beavers.

Mrs. Clarke said uncertainly, "I should have a word with Miss Lemon first."

"Dash it, Mrs. Clarke, you already told her

our plans," Butler said. "Jamie is sound asleep. He will never know you are gone."

She allowed herself to be led off. Renie asked if Colonel Jack had sent her a note. I told her he had not.

"Wouldn't you know! Now that I have some new gowns, I must sit at home." She continued in this vein for a moment, talking about the gowns and how she was modifying them.

While she was chatting, Professor Vivaldi bowed, put on his hat, and left. Renie's monologue did not require much in the way of attention. It left me free to see how Algernon reacted to my intransigence regarding the house. I expected lowering frowns and black looks, but he paid me no heed.

He just cast one speaking glance at Sharkey. Sharkey nodded his head almost imperceptibly and left. They did not exchange a single word, yet it was clear to me that Algernon had given a tacit command; Sharkey had acknowledged it—and gone off to do as he was bid. This pair was a well-oiled team, with Algernon the leader. I had a good idea what was going on. Sharkey was out to buy more stolen goods.

When we were alone, Algernon turned an accusing expression on me. "So, you have done it," he said. "Kicked the lot of us out on our ear."

I replied, "I have served notice that I mean to sell my house as soon as I find a buyer. In the meanwhile, if you and Sharkey bring any more stolen property into this house, I shall ask you to leave at once, before the house is sold."

"Me! Are you suggesting that I... ?"

"Yes, Lord Algernon, I am suggesting that you just gave Sharkey the nod to be about his business. You and he are in partnership, and I know which of you is in charge. You ought to be ashamed of yourself."

His jaws clenched, then he said through thin lips, "You misunderstood the matter, madam."

"I see. No doubt he is off buying another hunter for you. Or is his job this evening to follow a woman?"

It is difficult to describe his response to that charge. His face appeared to solidify into stone, yet his eyes were ablaze. "What the hell are you talking about?" he barked.

"I am talking about you using my house as a bawdy house and a den for stolen goods, sir. I will not have it, so don't bother trying to make me feel guilty for throwing the tenants out on their ears. It is bad apples like yourself who spoil it for others."

Strangely, he completely ignored the more serious charges. After swallowing his Adam's apple a couple of times he said, "What do you mean, following a woman?"

"You must tell Sharkey to lower his voice next time he is taking orders. But don't worry, I shan't tell Mrs. Clarke you are being unfaithful to her. There is some excuse for *her* behavior—though I do not hold her entirely innocent, either."

He stood perfectly still, while a look of the utmost conniving passed over his features. I could almost see his mind working feverishly to explain away his behavior. Whatever he said, I knew it would be a lie, to cover his shame.

Finally he said, "Whatever your opinion of me, Catherine, you traduce Mrs. Clarke to imply

135

she is honoring me with an affair. She is the sweetest, most innocent—"

"But with an odd taste in literature," I said.

"What are you talking about?" he asked warily.

"I went to her room to fetch Jamie's coral this afternoon for Miss Lemon. Or was the racy French novel by her bedside yours, Lord Algernon?"

His nostrils flared furiously, but he kept his voice low. "No, it was not mine. Perhaps it was Miss Lemon's," he said. "I daresay she has a lie down in Mrs. Clarke's room when Jamie is napping." This explanation had not occurred to me. I felt foolish at having accused him and Mrs. Clarke, until he said, "I happen to know for a fact that Anne does not speak French." That thoughtless "Anne" betrayed a greater closeness than he had shown before.

We glared at each other a moment, then he said, "Have you mentioned the French novel to anyone else?"

"No, why should I? I am not in the retail gossip business."

"You did not mention it to Renie when she was foraging for gowns?"

"I had not even seen the book then. Why are you worried about Renie? She knows perfectly well what is going on between you and Mrs. Clarke. She is the one—"

"You do not retail gossip; you just listen to it, eh, Miss Irving? And you take the word of that... actress over my word?"

"Why should I believe you? You have told me nothing but lies since the first time I met you." My temper soared along with my voice. "I want you to leave this house at once. Tonight!"

136

"Don't be so foolish," he said. Then he rammed his curled beaver on his head and stormed out the front door.

In his haste and anger, he forgot the door was freshly painted and must have smeared his fingers or coat, because I heard a string of accomplished oaths as the door slammed.

I sat on alone, trembling, and wishing I had not let all my anger come spilling out. It was worse than anger, it was jealousy. I had let myself become fond of Algernon, which was about the most foolish thing I could do. I would never marry a thief and lecher, and if he were an upright lord, he would not offer for someone like me. It was my inheriting this accursed house on Wild Street that had brought us together, and the sooner I was rid of it, the better.

Chapter Thirteen

It was a long, boring evening once the tenants had dispersed. I wondered what my aunt used to do in the evenings. It seemed strange to think that Mama's sister was satisfied to live in such a place as this. Miss Thackery found it odd that her friends did not call on us. Did she have any respectable friends? We decided that she must have become eccentric in her later years, because we could find no other explanation.

I found myself missing home, and Papa, and Radstock. On such fine evenings as this we used to go for a walk around the common and meet our friends. Children played noisily on the green, with the sheltering trees whispering secrets to the breeze while the crimson sun sank behind the spires of Papa's church. There were usually a few dogs around. Mrs. Stedmore's foolish tan spaniel, and one mongrel who liked to tease her. Sometimes we just sat on the benches gossiping and watching the ducks in the pond; other evenings if the wind grew chilly we would stop in for coffee at a neighbor's house.

On Wild Street, a lady dare not set her foot out the door after dusk without a male companion. The tall, dark houses with dusty windows looked menacing. I did not even want to think of what was going on behind those windows. Ruffians gathered on street corners, shouting and shoving one another, waiting for darkness, when they could go about their criminal pursuits. Any female who passed by was automatically taken for a streetwalker, and usually was one. Whatever her calling, she was subjected to catcalls and licentious jibes. Inebriates from the gin mills occasionally staggered by. It was obviously impossible for me to remain on here, and I had to wonder at the heaviness of my heart to think of leaving. But it was not Wild Street I minded leaving; it was Lord Algernon.

Mrs. Clarke and Mr. Butler were the first to return. They did not stop at the saloon, but ran upstairs chattering merrily.

"It is good to hear her laughing," Miss Thackery said. "She is too young and pretty to settle for a squalid flat on Wild Street. I wish Mr. Butler would take her home to his papa's house. That would be a better place for little Jamie to grow up."

Professor Vivaldi returned shortly after them. He stopped in to inquire if we would mind holding a parcel for him until it was picked up tomorrow. He was sending some books to a friend. Of course we agreed, and later he brought down the box and put it in the corner of the saloon, out of the way. Sharkey was next to arrive. If he was carrying any loot, he had it concealed beneath his jacket.

He came to the door and honored me with one of his crocodile smiles. "You are looking charming, as usual, if I may say so, Miss Irving," he said. "Too pretty to be sitting all alone." He began advancing with a rakish grin. Then he spotted Miss Thackery and quickly withdrew.

Bow Street did not come looking for him. We sat in the saloon with our needlework until ten-thirty, discussing whether we should send home for more clothes, or make do with what we had brought with us. Algernon had still not returned, and we decided to have a cup of cocoa and go to bed.

After an early night, I was up at seven-thirty the next morning. I heard the tenants leave, each off to his work. Except for Renie, of course, who "worked" nights if she worked at all. Mullard had to touch up the front door, which had been smeared with a dozen or so fingers. Miss Thackery went to the garden, and I tried to improve the looks of the interior of the house, to make it more enticing for buyers.

The tranter came for Professor Vivaldi's box of books. I wondered where he was sending them, for there was no address on the box, but the tranter said he knew the address and took them away. I went to the door to make sure he did not smear the paint. I had thought such a big box of books must be heavy, but the man carried it without any trouble. His wagon was already loaded with other boxes. All going to the same place, from the looks of them. At least they were all exactly the same, with letters and numbers stenciled on in black. A-D-L-1, A-D-L-2, and so on, about ten boxes in all.

Renie came down to show me how she had renovated one of Aunt Thalassa's gowns. She had done a good job of it, taking it in at the waist and lowering the neckline to show off her own opulent charms.

She stayed chatting awhile. When I said I wanted to remove the extra carpets, she offered to help. We called Mary, and the three of us removed the two top layers of carpet in the saloon. Renie took one up to her room, and Mary was happy to receive the other. She was going to have her brothers haul it home for her. The bottom carpet that remained was quite handsome, with flowers on a maroon and cream background.

We also moved the furniture about to find a more pleasing arrangement. When we were finished, Mary brought us tea, and Miss Thackery joined us.

"Do you think young Butler has screwed hisself up to the sticking point?" Renie asked, spooning in a quantity of sugar.

I said, "Asked Mrs. Clarke to marry him, you mean? I believe he is on the verge."

"There is a stroke of luck for her, then," Renie said. "His papa is well to grass, you must know. Five hundred acres in Devonshire, but unfortunately he is not the eldest son. Still, he should come into something when his pa sticks his fork in the wall."

I could not bring forth the name Mr. Alger when Miss Thackery was with us, but I noticed Renie did not make much of that affair. She appeared to think Mrs. Clarke would leap at an offer of marriage.

She continued, "I wish I had such an opportunity. I don't like to think what the future holds for the likes of me. I really don't. What will become of me now that I am getting long in the tooth and the producers don't want me?"

I felt this anxiety accounted for her overindulging in wine. It was indeed a bleak future for such women as Renie.

Miss Thackery said, "Do you not have any other skills than acting, Miss Whately?"

"I do, but I am getting a bit old for that, too. Jack did not call last night."

Miss Thackery cleared her throat discreetly and said, "You have done a fine job in making that gown of Mrs. Cummings's over. I hear they are looking for seamstresses at Covent Garden."

"You never mean it!" she exclaimed.

"Mary Freeman mentioned it. One of her sisters is thinking of applying. Mary has the advertisement with her in the kitchen now. Would you like to see it?"

"Lud, what good would that do me? I never could make any headway with letters. I always had to have someone teach me my lines, which is the only thing held me back from being a star, ladies, for I had the looks, I promise you. Just give me the name of that producer and I'll nip around to see him in person."

Miss Thackery rang for Mary to bring the advertisement, and soon Renie was heading off to Covent Garden.

"That is your good deed for the day," I complimented Miss Thackery. "I do feel sorry for my tenants. I dislike to leave them in the lurch. They seem so terribly vulnerable."

"You could take the ten-percent increase they offered, and give the management of the house over to an estate agent."

"Yes, I daresay I could do that."

"We could rent a nice set of rooms in Bath with the income, Cathy. I fear Mrs. Hennessey will be making headway with your papa while we are away. She must be lending him her carriage, don't you think?"

"Very likely."

"That will be an excuse for her to be running into the house a dozen times a day. She'll have an offer from him before we get home."

The afternoon passed in this quiet manner. Renie returned wreathed in smiles. She had gotten the job as a seamstress.

"I'll be head seamstress within the year," she assured us. "The old malkin who is designing the costumes now has no notion of how to please the gents. Gowns cut up to the collarbone. The producer just shook his head when I asked if they was putting on one of Hanna More's plays. He thinks they need a younger head seamstress," she added, with a sage nod.

"Mr. Davis will be calling on me later this evening, ladies, to chat about the costumes, you know," she continued. "I've just time to alter your aunt's violet silk. You wouldn't have a spare bottle of wine you could let me have?"

"I am sorry, Renie, but this is the last bottle. I should have ordered more."

She gave me an angry look. "That's odd. Your aunt always kept a good cellar."

"Mrs. Scudpole told me this was the last bottle."

"Do you mind if I have a look?"

"Go ahead."

She left, and was back in a few minutes, shaking her head. "You've been pilfered, ladies. Your cellar is as empty as my wallet. And I've a good notion who done it. Is Sharkey in?"

"Yes, he went upstairs."

She left, and I turned a fulminating eye on Miss Thackery. "That is what Sharkey was doing in the alley the first morning we were here. He had his wagon loaded and drove off with my wine under my very nose. I even heard the noise at the back door in the dead of night. I shall go up and demand he return it." I rose, ready to do battle.

Miss Thackery thought a moment, then spoke. "I shouldn't bother, Cathy. You have no proof, and we will soon be leaving here in any case. You would not want to haul the wine back to Radstock. Traveling is hard on wine, except for Madeira, I believe, which likes a good jostling. You would have to call in Bow Street, and take the case to court."

I sat down again, fuming in frustration. At six-thirty, we went to freshen up for dinner.

"It is odd Mrs. Clarke is not home. She is usually here by this time," Miss Thackery said.

"Perhaps she and Mr. Butler went looking at more flats."

We thought little of it. We sat down to dinner, the remains of the chicken served cold. We

143

were no sooner seated than Mary came to announce that Sharkey wanted a word with me.

"The man has no manners," Miss Thackery
scolded. "Did you tell him we are at the table,
Mary?"

"Yes, mum. He said it was urgent." Her eyes
were as big as saucers at such unusual goings on.

I feared he was in trouble with the law, but
if he thought for one instant I was going to abet
him, he was sorely mistaken. I would demand
that he return my wine, however.

I strode into the hallway, ready to rake his
hair with the closest chair. "What is it, Mr.
Sharkey?" I demanded sternly. His frightened
appearance suggested that he was indeed in
trouble.

"Have you heard from Mrs. Clarke?" he asked.
"She didn't come home. Miss Lemon is worried about her. She didn't say she would be
late. We thought she might have sent you a note."

"No, why would she notify me? I daresay she
and Mr. Butler are hunting for a flat before
darkness falls." His consternation appeared
greater than the situation called for. "It is not
yet seven o'clock, Mr. Sharkey. I shouldn't
worry."

"She isn't with Butler," he said. "He came
home alone. I went to the shop to get her. It
was closed. A sign on the door said OUT OF
BUSINESS."

My heard gave a jump of fear. "That's impossible! She went to work at the usual time
with Mr. Butler this morning."

"Yes, but he leaves her at the corner a block
from Lalonde's place. Demme, I wish Algie was
here."

"Perhaps she is with him," I said stiffly.

"No, he went to the House. I'd best go and tell him."

"It is a matter of particular concern to Mr. Alger?" I asked, with a pinched expression.

"He'd like to know," Sharkey replied discreetly.

"Then by all means, tell him." I noticed Algernon's interest was so keen that Sharkey had actually gone to the shop to escort Mrs. Clarke home, as if he were her bodyguard.

I was about to challenge Sharkey on the subject of wine when the front door opened, and Algernon came in. He looked at me; he looked at Sharkey—and apparently read our minds. "What is wrong?" he demanded.

"Mrs. Clarke is late getting home, and Mr. Sharkey thought you should know," I said, with a look of cool disdain. I had just managed to add two and two—and came up with the conclusion that Mrs. Clarke was the woman Sharkey was following for Algernon. My disdain was wasted on Algernon. He did not even notice it.

He looked like a wild man. "You were supposed to watch her!" he said to Sharkey.

"She never came out of the shop tonight, Algie. I waited a quarter of an hour, then went to the door and saw an OUT OF BUSINESS sign posted. A neighbor said it had been closed all afternoon, yet Anne went there this morning and never came home."

"Oh, God! Let me think!" It was a howl of outrage. I knew then that Mrs. Clarke was more than a bit of muslin for him. He was truly in love with her. My heart died a little, but I was

145

relieved that he had not made a plaything of the young widow. At least he was not that bad. Algernon shaded his eyes with his open hand and began walking in little circles, muttering to himself.

"Is there anything I can do?" I asked, for I truly wanted to ease his pain if I could.

Algernon looked up. "Has Vivaldi come home?"

"I don't know. I did not see him."

"Run up and knock at his door, Sharkey," Algernon said. "Make some excuse—you want to borrow some tea or milk." Sharkey was off like an arrow.

Algernon said to me, "Did you happen to mention to Vivaldi that Anne had that French book in her room?"

"No! Why would I do that?"

"No, of course you would not," he said distractedly.

"Algie, what is going on? What has Vivaldi to do with it?"

"I don't know. Perhaps nothing, but he does keep a very close eye on her."

"He wouldn't harm her. He is very fond of her."

Sharkey came bucketing downstairs, red in the face and out of breath. "He doesn't answer."

"We've got to get into his room," Algernon said. "He might have left some clue. Do you have a key for his room, Cathy?"

"I cannot let you into his room."

"This is a matter of life and death. Give me the key," he said through clenched jaws.

I got the key, but I went up with him to see he did not harm Vivaldi's room. I felt extremely guilty—and had no idea what excuse I would make if Vivaldi came home and caught us rooting through his private belongings. There was a sense of unreality about the whole affair. "A matter of life and death," Algie had said, and his grim manner told me it was no idle remark.

"What are we looking for?" I asked, as Sharkey and Algie moved around the room, looking in corners and opening drawers.

"I don't know," was Algie's unhelpful reply.

I saw a stack of classical books on the desk and picked one up. My fingers came away dusty. The whole desk was covered in a film of dust. He never used it at all. I opened the book and saw the stamp of a used bookstore. The books were all stamped with the same mark. He had picked up a bunch of used books to lend credence to his role of scholar. I pointed it out to Algernon. "He is not a scholar at all, is he?" I said.

"He might have been, once."

"What is he now? What is he doing here, on Wild Street?"

"Keeping an eye on Anne."

Sharkey called over his shoulder, "Take a look at this, Algie."

We both darted over to see what he had found. It was a passbook for a bank. Large sums of money, thousands of pounds, had been deposited and taken out again over the past six months.

"That's that then," Algernon said grimly. "He's got her. Keep looking. We'll tackle him when he comes back and beat the truth out of him."

The men kept searching the desk, opening

letters and glancing through them. Not knowing what we were looking for, I went to the bedroom. I noticed right away that it did not have the air of an occupied room. There was nothing on the toilet table, no brushes or combs. I went to the dresser and drew out the top drawer. It was empty, as were the others. Next I tried the clothespress. Vivaldi had removed every stitch of his clothing. It was empty.

I called into the parlor, "Come and look at this, Algie. I don't think Professor Vivaldi is coming back."

He turned and hurried across the floor to the bedchamber. "He's taken everything away," I said. "When did he do it? He did not leave with a trunk this morning."

"He didn't have much," Starkey said. "Always wore the same clothes."

"He must have had some linens at least," I said, and gave a gasp as I remembered that box of books. I told them about it.

"Did you happen to notice the address?" Algernon asked.

"There was no address. I mentioned it to the tranter. He said Vivaldi had told him where it was to go, but I didn't ask."

"What did the driver look like?" Algernon asked, or barked rather, for he was extremely upset.

"He wore a cap over his eyes. He was about forty or thereabouts, with an average sort of build. There was nothing to single him out from a thousand other workmen."

"Did you happen to notice anything about the carriage?" Sharkey asked.

"I hardly glanced at it, I fear. I did notice

that it was already well loaded. It had big card-board cartons on it. There was something printed on them."

"What? What were the words?"

"It wasn't whole words. Just letters, and I think some numbers. I can't remember. I'm sorry."

"Would the letters be A-D-L?" Sharkey asked.

"Yes! That's right. How did you know?"

"I've seen them before," he said, with a sly smile. Then he said to Algie, "They stand for Adele D. Lalonde. It's how all her goods for the shop are marked. She has smuggled silk shipped up from Kent, picks it up at the dock. Vivaldi used the same wagon to take away his belongings."

"That is odd. Surely it was not a coincidence," I said.

The men had forgotten I was there. They looked surprised when they turned and saw me, listening with both ears perked. "Algie, what is going on? Is Mrs. Clarke in danger?"

"She might very well be dead by now," he replied grimly. "Come on, Sharkey. I'll need your skills to break into the shop."

On this menacing speech they tore out of the flat. I heard them clattering down the stairs as I extinguished the candles and locked the door. Mrs. Clarke had been kidnapped. Her life was in danger, and presumably Algernon and Sharkey were going to Lalonde's Modiste Shop to try to rescue her. But I hadn't the least no-tion why anyone would kidnap a harmless young widow.

Chapter Fourteen

I went downstairs, confused and frightened, to find Miss Thackery, confused and angry, waiting for me.

"What on earth is going on, Catherine?" she demanded. I am only Catherine at moments of high drama, or when in disgrace. "Sharkey and Mr. Alger galloping through the house like a pair of colts, and you leaving your dinner half eaten—" Something in my face told her she was dealing with a more serious issue than poor manners. "What is it? What is the matter?" she demanded.

I drew her back into the dining room and closed the door. "Mrs. Clarke is missing," I said. "She did not come home from work. Algie thinks Professor Vivaldi has abducted her. Vivaldi has emptied his room and left."

"Good God!" she said, clutching at her heart. "Abducted that nice Mrs. Clarke! Are you sure it is not Mr. Butler who has her? It might be a runaway match."

"You are still thinking in terms of polite society, Miss Thackery. There is nothing to stop her from marrying Butler if she wishes. This is Wild Street. She has been abducted."

I told her the little I knew, and when she had digested that, we were reduced to speculation.

"Why would Vivaldi do such a thing? He never behaved like a satyr. You don't think he will harm her? You know what I mean… rape." The last word was a shiver of fear.

"Algie thinks she might already be dead," I said, and felt not only sorry and angry but guilty as well, for having traduced the woman.

I no longer thought she was Algie's mistress. Whatever was going on, it was not that. That was not why Sharkey followed her. It was to prevent her being kidnapped. And Mademoiselle Lalonde's shop was involved somehow.

We had a glass of wine to calm our nerves as we discussed the matter. I told Miss Thackery my suspicions, omitting any mention of a possible affair between the widow and Algernon. We tried to make sense of it, but it seemed a senseless business. She had no money, so it was not a kidnapping to hold her to ransom. What could a young widow be doing that would put her life in jeopardy? Her son meant the world to her; she would not endanger herself when Jamie depended on her.

"I was just thinking," Miss Thackery said, "that shop where she works, there must be Frenchies there, eh? The woman who runs it is Mademoiselle Lalonde. Could it have anything to do with spying? They say in the journals that London is full of French spies. She might be induced to do it, because of her husband being killed by the French. A sort of revenge. But Mrs. Clarke does not even speak French. I don't see how she could be learning anything there, unless she is stealing letters, or some such thing."

I thought of that French novel by her bed, and her insistence the first time we met that she did not speak French. She obviously did, but did not want anyone to know it. The French staff and customers at Lalonde's would speak

151

freely in front of her if they thought she could not understand them. "I think she does speak French, or read it at least," I said, and mentioned the French novel as evidence.

"You never told me that, Cathy."

"It did not seem important."

"And Algernon is in on it, you think? I am surprised he would put that poor girl in such jeopardy."

"Let us not judge him too harshly until we know all the facts." I had learned one lesson from this experience at least.

Miss Thackery's next notion was that Wild Street was too treacherous for such greenheads as us, and we must remove to a hotel at once.

"We might be able to help in some way," I countered. "I shall stay, but if you—"

"It was you I was thinking of, Cathy. No one would harm an old lady like me."

We finished our wine and went to the saloon to await news. It seemed a very long time before Algernon and Sharkey returned—alone. I went darting to the saloon door to ask if they had found her. Their grim faces made me fear they had discovered her corpse, but it was not quite that bad.

"No one was at the shop. Sharkey got the back door open for us," Algie said vaguely. I assumed breaking into locked houses was no new thing for Sharkey. "Anne's bonnet and pelisse were gone, but she had left her reticule behind, so she had been there all right."

Sharkey was carrying her black patent bag. As he held it out to show us, there was a gasp of horror. Turning, we saw Miss Lemon in the doorway. "That is her reticule!" she said, rushing forward. "Mr. Alger... have you found her?"

"Not yet, Miss Lemon," he said quietly, "but we shan't stop until we do."

"She is dead! I know it. Oh, I told her she should not do it! It was too dangerous."

Algie hurried forward to speak quietly to her, with his back to us to shield his words. I realized that Miss Lemon knew precisely what her mistress was up to. I felt that Algernon had hired her to help protect Mrs. Clarke. They spoke for a moment, then asked for the reticule. They searched it for clues, but apparently found nothing. When Miss Lemon went back upstairs to watch Jamie, she took the reticule with her.

Algie turned to me. "Vivaldi has not returned, of course?"

"No, and he won't. Algie, have you no idea at all where she can be?" He looked at me and Miss Thackery uncertainly, as if he would like to take us into his confidence.

"We know what is going on," I said. "Mrs. Lalonde's shop was some sort of French spy center, and Mrs. Clarke was spying on them."

"So you figured it out. Well, it is true. Anne never told them that she speaks French. They assumed she did not—and used to discuss their business in front of her from time to time. She soon realized they were spies and came to Whitehall to volunteer her services. We wanted her to quit the job. We would send in an older, more experienced woman to take over. Mrs. Clarke would not hear of it. She put us on to a few things."

"Did they ever mention any other place—

153

one of their homes or whatnot—where they might have taken her?"

"There was only Mademoiselle, who is in fact Madame Lalonde, and her husband, Alfonse Lalonde. Or at least they lived together as man and wife. He handled the deliveries and accounts and so on. Madame Lalonde did the designing and fitting; Anne helped with the sewing. The Lalondes lived above the shop. It is empty as well."

"Then you have no idea where she might be?"

"Not at the moment, but we shan't give up. I know a few cafés where the Frenchies hang out in the evenings. Sharkey has been helping me. There is one club where Alfonse goes fairly regularly. He might be there, and if not, Sharkey can direct us to a few of his close friends. I'll haul them off for questioning."

"Why do you think they abducted her at this time, if she has been there six months without suspicion?"

He replied, "Anne thought they were becoming suspicious of her. The last information she brought me was a false clue. I think they were testing her. Alfonse was supposed to be meeting a contact at Hyde Park at eleven o'clock at night. We know they are getting information from someone at the Horse Guards, an English traitor. Naturally we are eager to discover who he is. I went along to try to see the contact, but he never came. I don't think Alfonse saw me, but perhaps they had another man looking out for me. If I was seen, then they know that Anne tipped me off. She was certain they did not know she spoke French, but I fear Vivaldi tumbled to it somehow. That is why he moved in here, to watch her."

"Perhaps he saw that French book when he took Jamie the tin soldiers."

"She was a little careless about leaving her books around, but she had so few visitors it did not seem important. If Vivaldi called, then it was for the purpose of snooping around. No doubt he spotted something."

"I wish you could have convinced her to quit when you thought they mistrusted her," I said, not in accusation but in frustration.

"So do I; she was adamant. I did tell her that if any such thing as this happened, she must tell them to contact Lord Dolman, who will pay handsomely for her release. She is to claim kinship with him. Greed is a strong incentive. I doubt they would kill her without trying for the money. That will buy us some time. Papa will send the note to me at once if it comes."

"Would he actually pay for her safety?" I asked.

"The Horse Guards do provide funds for such contingencies, but the idea is to use the money as a bait to catch the spies." Algernon rose and said, "We must be going now. I only came back to let Miss Lemon know what is afoot. You might go up and spend some time with her if you want to help, ladies. This is a hard time for her to be alone."

"Yes, of course we shall take care of Miss Lemon."

He smiled a sad little smile, the kind of smile that made me wish we were alone. It was intimate, tender, loving. "Be careful, Algie," I said.

"We'll keep in touch. You must be cursing me for making you stay on here. But we had things so cozily arranged, with Sharkey and

155

myself to look out for Mrs. Clarke—and Butler always on hand to help out, though he hasn't a notion what is going on. It seemed a shame to disrupt it. What we did not know was that Vivaldi was a part of the ring. He came a month ago. For that long, they have suspected her."

"Wouldn't surprise me if he's French," Sharkey said. "Letting on he's Italian gives an excuse for his funny accent."

"You are probably right," Algernon said. Then he looked at his watch and hauled Sharkey away.

"What a wretched state of affairs," Miss Thackery said. "I shall go up and sit with Miss Lemon now. She must be distracted. Will you come with me, Cathy?"

"I shall be up shortly. I just want to sit quietly a moment and see if I can remember anything that might help. If Vivaldi ever said anything, you know, or... I don't know. I just want to think."

Rational thought was impossible, of course. My mind was too full of horrible possibilities: Anne alone with those wicked Frenchies who would not deal kindly with an English spy; poor Jamie, not only fatherless but motherless as well. And I thought of how brave young Anne was. She seemed the softest, gentlest girl in all of England, and all the time there was a tiger's heart lurking in her breast. Algie had warned her she was in jeopardy, but she would not stop as long as there was hope of retaliating for her husband's death. How she must have loved her James!

I was not alone long. Within five minutes, Mr. Butler came downstairs, looking worried. "Mrs. Clarke is still not back from work, Miss

Irving. Have you heard from her? Very likely she is working overtime. She does that once in a while. Perhaps I should go down to the shop to walk her home. I mean—" He stopped, staring at me. "Something has happened to her," he said in a hollow voice. His ruddy face turned paper white.

Mr. Butler would have to know the whole soon enough. He was Mrs. Clarke's closest friend. She might have told him things she had not even told Algie. It was unlikely, but he might possibly be able to shed some light on the disappearance.

I invited him to sit down and said as gently as I could that Mrs. Clarke had vanished—and we thought Mademoiselle Lalonde and Professor Vivaldi had abducted her.

"That foul old wretch! I knew he had his rheumy old eyes on her, bringing Jamie toy soldiers!"

"I do not think that was his reason, Mr. Butler. It has to do with the Frenchies at the shop. The war..."

He sat trembling, unable to speak. "I always knew there was something—she had some secret. About her speaking French, for instance. Her Bible is in French, and I once saw her reading it. She said she refused to speak French in public, or even admit she knew it, because the French had killed her husband. Why did she not tell me what she was up to? I might have helped her. To put herself in such danger!"

"Can you think of anything else she said that might help us find her, Mr. Butler? Did she ever mention any names of people who came into the shop."

"She had to make a gown for Caro Lamb once."

"Not just customers, but other people. Frenchmen," I said, to make myself clear.

"She never talked about the shop much," he said. "Mostly she talked about her husband and Jamie. Lately, though, she had begun to get over his death, I think. When you put the notice up about selling the house, we agreed we would both move into the same house again, if we could. I hoped, of course, that we might live together as man and wife. I think I had half talked her into it. At least she let me call her Anne. We found a dandy little flat on Tavistock Street. Too expensive for one of us, but if we pitched in... Mind you, she did not accept an offer of marriage, but she did not say no, either."

"And you cannot think of anything at all that might help us find her?"

"No, but demme, I'll find her if I have to tear London apart stone by stone." He flung his arms about as he spoke.

To try to assuage his rising hysteria, I explained Algernon's plans for her rescue and suggested that he might be able to help in some manner, but he must stay calm, for Anne's sake. I poured him a glass of wine and sat with him, waiting for Algernon to return.

Chapter Fifteen

I have no doubt the saloon on Wild Street has seen some strange things in its day, but I doubt it ever saw stranger goings-on than it saw that night. I had just convinced Butler he must eat to keep up his strength and sent him to our dining room for some of Mary's chicken, when Algernon returned, alone and in a high state of excitement.

He peered in at the saloon door to see if I was alone before he exclaimed, "I have the ransom note!" He held it out in his hand to show me. "I called on Papa to tell him what had happened. He had just received the note."

"What does it say?" I asked, jumping up to examine it.

It was written on a piece of cheap white paper. "That is Vivaldi's writing," Algernon said. "I have seen it on your bulletin board."

The note was brief and to the point:

Five thousand pounds in gold coins. You have until noon tomorrow. Details for exchange following. If you want to see Mrs. Clarke alive, do not go to police.

"How do we know she is not already dead?" I asked.

He handed me another note, written on a piece of paper torn from the top of that same evening's journal, bearing the printed date to prove when it was written. I opened it, and a lock of Anne's hair fell into my palm. That little blond curl caused my stomach to clench in a knot. I cringed to think of that poor girl, so vulnerable at the hands of those thugs. Why had they cut her beautiful hair? It seemed a wanton and cruel act of vandalism. The note was in her own hand, but her nervous condition made the writing wobbly. It said:

Algernon: I am alive and well. Please do as they say, and take care of Jamie for me.

159

"Are you certain this is her writing?" I asked.

"I am fairly sure. I do not think they would kill her when she is worth five thousand pounds to them alive."

I looked again at that pathetic little blond curl. "Don't let Butler see this. Why did they cut her hair?"

"As proof that they have her, I suppose. And to strike fear into our hearts. If they can cut her hair... they can cut her throat," he said grimly.

"Oh, Algernon! We must rescue her! Five thousand pounds! Can you get the money by noon tomorrow?"

"Papa is arranging it now. Of course I shall try to recover Anne before then, preferably without putting five thousand in Boney's coffers. Sharkey has not returned?"

"Not yet."

"Then he has run into trouble. He should have been back before me. The gin mill favored by the French is not far from here."

We had very little time to talk. Our conversation was all about Anne's safety and how we could recover her. Algernon told me he and Sharkey had searched the shop and the rooms above it thoroughly. There had been nothing indicating where they might have gone.

"They did not remove their few furnishings, so there was no hope of anyone noticing where the tranter's wagon went," he explained. "Lalonde's shop was little more than a pied-à-terre. The parcels you saw on the wagon Vivaldi used were not at the shop. They were delivered to one of the other shops, I expect. We think, Papa and I, that the French have a series of them around the city. The Lalondes are small fish, probably reporting to one man in charge of the whole. This affair was planned in advance."

"I wonder who this man could be."

"We cannot say, but one thing Papa did find out. There was no Professor Vivaldi ever at Oxford. That is the background Vivaldi claimed for himself. He is a cultured gentleman. From the two times I played chess with him, I can tell you he has a formidable brain. I am counted a better-than-average player, but I hadn't a chance against him. He mentioned belonging to a chess club in London. We think he may have made his contact with the British traitor there. A certain Clarence Makepiece is under surveillance. We have not been able to catch him yet, but he will be questioned more severely now."

"Vivaldi was out of his rooms all day," I said. "No doubt he was visiting his minions, collecting their gleanings and brewing up mischief against our troops."

"I feel the same. This is my chance to get him," he said, with a grim smile.

The front door flew open, and Sharkey came in. "Not a sign of any of them," he announced. "Milkins's gin mill was half empty. Milkins told me none of the Frenchies had been in all day. They've been tipped off to make themselves scarce."

Algernon muttered a few profanities into his collar and smacked his closed fist against my desk in frustration.

Sharkey said primly, "*Tsk*, Algie. There is a lady present." He honored me with one of his crocodile smiles before turning back to Algernon. "Don't give up. I've put the word out on the nappy lads' grapevine. Every prigger and bung nipper and ruffler and bawd in the neighborhood will be after the reward. I had to offer a reward," he said, peering for signs of objection. "I hope you're good for ten guineas. Anybody seeing anything will get back to me here pronto."

"Cheap at the price," Algernon said.

"What are priggers and those bung people, Mr. Sharkey?" I asked in confusion.

"They are various sorts of rogues," Algernon said vaguely.

"Your priggers and rufflers are thieves," Sharkey explained. "Your bung nipper is a file."

"A file?"

"Pickpocket," Algernon explained.

I did not have to inquire what a bawd might be. I said faintly, "But why are these—people—coming here, to my house?"

"I told them to watch their tongues and act proper, knowing you're a lady," Sharkey said.

"Naturally they are welcome if they can help find Anne, but they are not involved with the French—are they?"

"Certainly not! They're as patriotic as John Bull, but they know more about what's going on in London than all the journals and politicians put together," Sharkey told me. "They spend their days and nights on the streets with their ears and eyes open. They have to be sharp to live. If anybody leaves a house empty, they know about it. An empty house is a place to lay down indoors for a night, as well as maybe pick up a few gewgaws. I wager Lalonde's shop

162

is picked clean by now of any ribbons or buttons she left behind. There'll be half a dozen lads camping there until somebody else moves in."

"You have already checked Lalonde's shop," I said.

"That was just an example, you might say," Sharkey said. "Get a bunch of the nappy lads together and they might know not only that the crew left, but where they went. That's what we're after."

"I see!"

"And there's the prancer priggers," Sharkey added, slipping into cant again.

"Horse thieves," Algernon explained.

"They know every piece of horseflesh to be seen on the streets of London, along with every cabdriver. Jocko is our lad for prancers. The Lalondes didn't have a rig, so they must have used a hansom cab to move Mrs. Clarke. And there's Vivaldi to think of as well. He didn't vanish into thin air. Ten to one he took a cab to wherever he's hiding. I put out an emergency call for Jocko."

"Well done," Algernon said.

It was not long before the door knocker sounded. Sharkey peered through the curtains and said, "It's a Drury Lane vestal. Spotty Meg, I believe."

The female was a common bawd. The sobriquet Spotty Meg might have been an unkind reference to her complexion, which bore the ravages of smallpox, or it might have referred to her gown, which wore a few months dirt on its silken surface. She was stout and jolly. Her age was uncertain; whether she was an aged

163

thirty or a young forty I could not tell. The only gray on her coppery hair was dust.

"Sharkey, luv," she said, sidling up to him while peering uncertainly at me from the corner of a flashing black eye, "I hear there's something in it for any mort who's seen that fellow calls hisself Professor Vivaldi."

"For anybody that can put a finger on him," Sharkey said. "He's disappeared."

"Tip me a dace and I might be able to tell you something," Meg said, with a leer.

Sharkey gave her tuppence, which she stored in her bodice. She looked longingly at the wine. I poured her a glass and offered her a chair. "Thankee ever so, dear." She smiled, then proceeded with her tale.

"He was a strange cove, the professor," she said. "I knew he was up to something, the way he nipped and capered about. What he'd do, he'd walk out of this house each morning quite early, down Keane Street to Aldwych. A solicitor, I figured, going to the Inns of Court. I got to wondering why a decent businessman lived here, so I followed him one day, thinking there might be something in it for me. Hiding from a wife or debtors, I figured." She took a swig of the wine and wiped her mouth with the back of her hand.

"Well, sir, he hops into a carriage and darts off in t'other direction, west along the Strand. It made me curious, like, why he'd walk one way, then drive t'other, so I followed him a couple of more times. Took the same crinkum-crankum route every day, he did. That cove's up to something, I says to myself."

"Did he meet anyone?" Algernon asked.

164

"Not a soul. He kept hisself to hisself. He wasn't one to give a girl a tumble. I used to see him coming back at night, too. I walked along to the same spot where he got into his rig in the morning—and didn't he get out of it at six o'clock and walk home by the same crooked route. What do you make of that, eh?"

"Could you describe the carriage?" Sharkey asked.

"A good rattler, but not flashy. Plain black. A groom but no footman. A team of bays."

Sharkey said, "Send Jocko in if you see him. Put out the word."

"Jocko's your man for prads," Meg said, and finished her wine.

Algernon handed her a coin that put a broad smile on her face. "Why, thank you ever so," she said. She put the coin in her gown to keep her tuppence company and left. "Back to the streets," she said, patting her bosom contentedly.

"What do you make of that?" Algernon said when she had gone.

"Jocko might know something about the rattlers and prads," Sharkey said.

I said, without thinking, "Does she work day *and* night? I had thought her... profession... would work at night, but she seems to be on the streets all day as well."

"Spotty Meg'll turn her hand to anything," Sharkey explained. "She's not a specialist. A bit of a pinch artist—picks up small items in shops; she'll even nab the snow when her regular business is slow. Take linen off clotheslines," he explained when I looked at him in confusion.

165

"She is very... versatile," I said, trying not to sound condemnatory.

"Yes." Algernon smiled. "I hope you were not too attached to that little china bowl that used to be on your desk."

I looked—and saw Miss Thackery's dish of peppermints had vanished. "She even took the peppermints!"

"Better count your fingers, Algie," Sharkey said, and laughed at Meg's prank. "I told her to behave proper. I'll get the dish back for you, Miss Irving."

"Never mind. She needs it worse than I."

Our next callers were a pair of ken crackers named Silent Sam and Noisy Ned. They worked as a team to break into houses and rob them. Noisy Ned created a diversion in front of the house by dropping to the ground and pretending to have taken a convulsion. Silent Sam would come along and pose as a doctor, as a ploy to get into the house chosen for pilfering. Sam would send the servants off for wine or other medications, and they would both pick up any small valuables while they were alone. They waited until the master and mistress had left the house before their performance. The servants, it seemed, were more easily gulled.

One would think, to look at Sam and Ned, that they were respectable gentlemen. They wore decent blue jackets and were clean enough. A closer look revealed the shifty eyes and sly grin of the rogue. They reverted to their true form with Sharkey.

"Word is out you're interested in Lalonde's place," Ned said. Sam was indeed silent. We scarcely heard a word from him. "Me and Sam

166

paid a call round around two, when the place had been empty an hour or more. Honest Eddie has taken over for the night. He's set up a friendly card game with a couple of well-in-laid flats from the country.

"What did you find in there?" Sharkey asked.

Sam, though silent, found a mode of communicating. He held up his right hand and rubbed his thumb against his fingers, to indicate he wanted payment for his information.

"Let's hear what you've got to say first," Sharkey said.

Ned drew a list from his pocket and read. " 'An ell of sprigged muslin, yellow. Half an ell ditto, pink. A hank of green silk—not enough for a gown but for a shawl. Six yards satin ribbon—' "

Sharkey waved him to silence. "We don't want an inventory, Ned. Was there anything in the way of a map, a letter, an address...?"

"Clean as a whistle, that way. Account books gone, money box empty. Desk emptied. Done a flit, we figured. No point letting the bailiff nab the goods."

"That news ain't worth listening to," Sharkey told him. "But here's something for your trouble. If you see Jocko, send him along. I'm anxious to see Jocko." He handed Ned some small coins.

Since Sharkey paid him, I did not hesitate to ask Sam to return the silver-framed picture of my aunt Thalassa's late husband, which he had lifted from the desk while Ned entertained us. He drew it from his pocket with a sly grin.

"Now how did that get in there?" he said. They were the only words he spoke during the whole visit.

I did not notice until later that either he or Spotty Meg had gotten away with the silver-plated ink pot. "How could they steal it? It was full of ink!" I exclaimed.

Sharkey pointed to a half glass of wine I had left on the desk. It was now full of a deep blue ink wine.

"Those fellows are wasting their time. They ought to set up as magicians. Unfortunately I cannot bring up a new bottle of wine," I said, staring at Sharkey. "Mine has mysteriously vanished from the cellar."

"There's rats in that cellar," Sharkey said.

"Do they know how to draw a cork?"

We were interrupted by another visitor, a "cove" whose job description was jarkman. His line of crime was to falsify documents, but he had not done so for Vivaldi or any of the others. He offered to forge documents proving me a French countess for two guineas, or a duchess for three. I declined.

"An Italian contessa," he ventured. I shook my head.

"P'raps it's just as well. You don't look like a foreigner. That face is as English as suet pudding. If you ever feel the need to drop a decade from your age, I can print you up a birth certificate quick as winking. It would fool any judge in the country."

"But would it fool the gentlemen?" Sharkey asked, and gave a playful laugh. "Just fooling, Miss Irving. You are still as fresh as spring lamb."

"Thank you, I shall bear the offer in mind when I turn to mutton."

"That won't be for half a decade yet," Sharkey assured me.

I thought the house had escaped depredations from the jarkman until I went into the hallway to answer the next knock and saw the umbrellas were gone. There had been three umbrellas in a large blue-and-white vase when the evening began. I removed the vase, took down the painting from the wall, and decided that if anyone wanted the ragged runner on the floor, he was welcome to it.

I opened the door, and a person whom I first mistook for a boy hopped in. A closer look showed me he was an extremely small man with a lined face, very few teeth, and no hair whatsoever when he removed his hat. A fringe of dark hair had been attached to the hat's rim by some means, but it came off with the hat.

"I hear the Shark is looking for me," he said, with a toothless grin.

"Whom shall I say... ?"

"Jocko, miss. Just Jocko. He'll know."

"Jocko!" I grabbed him by the lapels and made him welcome. "Come in. We have been waiting for you."

He flicked my fingers away with a sharp look and smoothed his tatty lapels. I noticed the fingers were out of his gloves, but they had once been good gloves. York tan, at least two sizes too large for Jocko.

"If you will just step this way," I said.

His eyes toured the empty hallway, then he fell in behind me.

Chapter Sixteen

Sharkey came darting into the hall to meet Jocko. "Good lad! It took you long enough to get here."

Jocko replied, "I blush to confess I came on shank's mare. Me! The best prancer prigger in the country! Can you believe it?" He slid into the saloon.

"It's a rare day when Jocko's feet tread the cobblestones. What happened?"

"A few of the lads set up a card game with a pair of Johnny Raws from the country. I was to relieve them of their prads while Captain Sharp lightened their pockets. Turned out the coves were fly. They came in a hired cab, brought their own cards and wine, and have guns in their pockets. The game is at Lalonde's abandoned shop. I was just on my way to tell Spotty Meg. She might want to have a go at them. They didn't bring their own lightskirts at least."

"She'll hear about it. This is more important."

He led Jocko to a comfortable chair. I brought him a glass and what remained of the wine.

Jocko looked at the decanter with disdain and said, "Would you have a drop of brandy at all?"

"I am afraid not," I replied.

"Bottom shelf of the sideboard, left, behind the cups," Sharkey informed me. "I used to keep your aunt supplied, Miss Irving," he explained, when I looked my astonishment.

I brought the brandy. Before I could pour a

glass, Jocko reached out and took the bottle. He poured himself a large glass and smacked his lips.

"Nectar of the gods!" He smiled his toothless smile and drank. "It is strange a race that eats frogs has such good taste in drink. Now, what can I do for you, Sharkey?"

"A cove called Vivaldi used to leave this house every morning and meet a carriage at the corner of Aldwych and Drury Lane, somewhere around there."

"Just so, the long drink of water—a foreigner. A professor, I think he called hisself?"

"That's right, Vivaldi."

"Plain black rig, a decent team of bays. Not bloods by any means, but a gentleman's team. The wagon was his own. He hired the prancers from Booter's stable on Eagle Street, near Gray's Inn. What do you want to know about him?"

"He's disappeared. We want to find him. If you happen to know where he used to go in that rig, it'd be worth something," Algernon said.

"I have reason to believe he was a salesman of some sort. He carried a black case, used to make regular stops at certain shops specializing in ladies' goods and toys."

"Could you give us a list of those shops?" Algernon asked, with a gleam in his eyes. This would be Vivaldi's network of spies.

"I would have to drive the route. I cannot recall them offhand, but I'd recognize them to see them right enough. I never actually followed the professor. No reason to. His man never left the nags unattended, but I used to see the rig coming and going as I made my usual rounds."

"Good! We'll do the tour tomorrow. For the moment, we are interested to discover where that team of bays is now."

"I can tell you that," Jocko said. "They are back at Booter's stable. I was there, selling Booter a dandy ladies' mount I prigged from a private stable when the groom brought the prads in this afternoon. He hired a stronger team of four. Looks like he plans a trip. He would not need four for town."

"He's making a dart for France, since we've rumbled his game," Sharkey said to Algernon.

"Some havey-cavey business, is there?" Jocko inquired, with mild interest, as he sipped the brandy. "Am I correct in deducing it is the cove you are interested in, not the team?"

"That's the idea," Sharkey said. "If he hires the nags, Booter must have an address for him."

"The address he left is Wild Street," Jocko said, but he said it with an extremely cagey grin. "Which is not where you will find him."

"Do you know where he is? Name your price!" Algernon said.

A blissful smile seized Jocko's face at such a naive utterance. "I do, sir. I happened to over-hear Booter ask the lad how he liked St. John's Wood. From the conversation, I deduced the professor goes there on weekends. I have a certain ladyfriend— But you are not interested in that. Suffice it to say I have seen the professor driving in that direction, usually on a Sunday, when I visit my Bessie."

Algernon was out of his chair. "Have you any idea where in St. John's Wood?"

"I have, sir. I know the very house. As soon

as we have settled on a price. Shall we say... twenty guineas?"

Sharkey said, "Twenty guineas! You're out of your head. Ten."

"This is no time to quibble. Twenty it is," Algernon said, and pulled Jocko out of his chair.

"Let us just see the readies," Jocko said.

Algernon emptied his pockets, and Jocko snatched the money. "I happened to overhear Booter ask him if he had seen any of the balloon ascents that take place in St. John's Wood. The lad said he had watched one from his own window last Sunday. Now where would that be but the empty field at the corner of Abbey Road and Grove End Road? I could show you the very house. If there will be either fisticuffs or shooting, you must hold me excused from participating," he said. "I supply information only, not physical support... except in the way of a prancer."

"Take Butler, Algie," I said. "He will be eager to go with you."

"We could use an extra man. We don't know how many of them are there," Sharkey said.

"Very well. Tell him to hurry."

I darted to the dining room, where Butler was sitting with Mary, talking about Anne. Mary's eyes were moist, and Butler's were not far from it.

"Come along, Mr. Butler. We think we have discovered where Anne is," I said.

He was up like a shot and went pelting into the saloon to join Algernon and Sharkey.

"Do you have guns?" I asked.

"Do dogs have fleas?" was Sharkey's reply.

"For God's sake, be careful," I gasped, gripping Algernon's fingers. Lack of time and privacy robbed us of a decent parting. I suddenly found there were so many things I wanted to say to him. I might never see him again. I wanted to apologize for our many arguments… and to tell him I loved him.

"Put on a kettle," Sharkey said. "I'll have him back safe before you can say Jack Robinson."

"My dear," Algernon said, and lifted my hand to his lips. "Thank you… for everything." His eyes glowed with emotion, saying all the things we could not say. Then they were gone, and I was left with the lady's onerous chore of waiting, while poor Anne and the man I loved were in danger.

I went upstairs to tell Miss Lemon and Miss Thackery the latest development. They were greatly cheered, though of course not totally relieved until Anne was safely home. I returned belowstairs to intercept any other callers who might come to relieve me of my goods and chattels—and to ponder on this other half of humanity of whose existence I had scarcely been aware before coming to Wild Street.

I had always known, in an intellectual way, that there were cutpurses and horse thieves and prostitutes and such people in the world, but as I had never met them before, they were a faceless tribe—the stuff of fiction. Now that I had actually been confronted with them, I found myself more sympathetic than condemnatory. As badly off as my tenants were, these petty criminals were worse. They lived hand-to-mouth, lurking about the streets like stray dogs, doing what they must to survive another day.

Still, I was frightened to be alone downstairs with such questionable callers coming to the door, so I sent for Mullard to join me. Even before he arrived, another caller came. It was another Drury Lane vestal. This one was called Florie, and she was much too young to be on the streets. About sixteen, I judged, with her charms still intact. She was a small blond girl.

"I come about Sharkey's message, miss," she said, curtsying awkwardly.

"Mr. Sharkey has left, but if you have any information, you can tell me."

"I seen him and Jocko leave. I was waiting outside, screwing up my courage to come in." Her hands were clenching her skirt in nervousness as she spoke. "I seen them take the modiste away, miss. They had her wrapped in a blanket. I only thought she was sick."

"What time was this?"

"Oh, it was hours ago, miss. If I'd know anything was wrong, I'd of come sooner."

"Did you see where they took her?"

Tears began streaming down her cheeks. "No, miss. They put her in a carriage. She wasn't struggling or nothing. It was a black carriage. She ain't kilt, is she? Her with the little baby?"

"No, we think she will be all right. They have—" I decided it was wiser to keep my own counsel.

The girl looked at me with eyes as big as saucers—such pretty, innocent eyes. "They've gone after her?" she asked sharply.

I immediately smelled a plot and said, "No. They have gone on other business. It has nothing to do with Mrs. Clarke."

She heaved a sigh of relief. "That's good then.

What I came to tell you, miss—one of the men who put the modiste in the carriage was lurking outside the house, watching the comings and goings. Alfonse, it was. He's Madame Lalonde's fancy man. He followed Mr. Alger's rig, but if it has nothing to do with the modiste—"

I felt as if the bottom had fallen out of my stomach. Alfonse had been spying on the house! He was following Algernon, no doubt with a pistol in his pocket.

"Miss, are you all right?" Florie said.

I willed down the panic that was rising up in me. "I am fine, thank you, Florie. Here is something for your trouble." I gave her a guinea.

"Oh, thank you, miss. I never had a whole guinea before."

It was such a pathetic speech that it penetrated even through my other emotions. "Come back tomorrow, Florie," I said. I had some vague notion of reforming her, but it was just a fleeting thought.

She left, clutching her guinea and thanking me a dozen times. I ran toward the kitchen and met Mullard just coming to join me.

"What is amiss?" he demanded when he saw my ashen face.

"We have to go after Algernon and warn him he is being followed."

Mullard looked totally confused, and I realized he was unaware of all that had passed that evening. But there was no time to tell the tale.

"Harness up the carriage at once, Mullard. I shall tell you all about it on the road."

I ran for my bonnet and pelisse, with my heart throbbing in my throat and my stomach quaking. I knew I should tell Miss Thackery, and I knew as well that she would not want me to go. I told Mary to tell her, after I had left, that I had to go out on an emergency. I wished with all my heart that I had a pistol. We did not keep one in the carriage.

It had been discussed before we left home, but Papa had not thought it wise or necessary. I grabbed up the poker and ran to wait at the door, because I could not sit still. A single second saved might make the difference.

The few minutes' wait seemed an eternity, but at last the carriage came, and I darted out into the shadows.

Chapter Seventeen

"Where are we headed, miss?" Mullard asked, holding the carriage door for me.

"St. John's Wood. Hurry."

"Which way is that, then?"

I stopped dead in my tracks, one foot on the carriage step, one on the ground. "I don't know."

I had not given it a single thought until that moment. I only knew that Algernon was in danger, and I must go to him. Saint John's Wood might as well have been Tombouctou, as far as Mullard and I were concerned. We hadn't a notion of how to reach it.

"The map," Mullard said, and hopped up to the perch to fetch it.

We read it by the light of the carriage lamps. It took us an age to locate St. John's Wood in the upper left-hand corner, nearly off the map. "It looks very far away," I said, my heart sinking.

"Aye, but pretty straightforward," Mullard pointed out.

We went over the directions a couple of times until we had memorized them. Once we were on Oxford Street, we felt we knew what we were about. It was getting to Oxford Street that was more difficult. The map was a veritable maze of streets, none of which appeared to be where they should when we were actually driving. Mullard had to stop twice to ask directions, and both times I was in an agony of impatience. I wished I could sprout wings like a bird and fly above all the busy thoroughfares.

We did eventually find Oxford Street, however, and when we had finally turned on to Edgeware Road, the traffic was light enough that I felt I could in decency join Mullard on the box to tell him what was going on. Talking about it helped to ease the anxious thoughts crowding my mind. The wind and the open sky above helped, too. I had felt like a prisoner, locked alone with my fears in the dark carriage.

"You shouldn't ought to have come, missie," Mullard said, when I had apprised him of the situation. "Nor would I have brought you, if I'd known what mischief you were up to. I could have come alone. I fear to think what your papa will say when he hears."

"He shan't hear of it from me, Mullard."

We exchanged a small conspiratorial smile. "Nor from me, unless I have to report your death. Which I won't. You'll stay in the carriage while I go after Lord Algernon to warn him."

"If we are not too late. We have no hope of overtaking him with these tired old nags."

"Nay, the nags are fresh as daisies," he said,

whipping the team up as fast as they could go. Mullard had set a good pace once we hit the open road. "They may never make it home, but they're fast enough on a shortish haul."

The traffic grew thinner and the trees thicker as we proceeded farther from town. At times we drove through a veritable forest; at other times, we had a vista of starlit meadows. Occasionally we spotted a carriage ahead. Mullard would whip up the team, but the few rigs we managed to pass were heavy country carriages. We saw no trace of either Alfonse or Algernon. There was a sign announcing St. John's Wood. The area was still well wooded, but with the city beginning to reach its tentacles out in the form of houses and some commercial buildings. At Grove End Road Mullard turned left.

"You might keep your eyes peeled for Abbey Road now," he said. "'Tis less than half a mile away, according to our map."

"I doubt Algernon would have driven up to the door. His carriage will be parked somewhere along here, in a laneway or under a cluster of trees."

"We'll do likewise. You get in the rig. I'll ankle along and find the house."

"I cannot stay here alone, Mullard! Some prancer prigger might come along to steal the horses. I would be safer with you."

"Where did you pick up such language!" he exclaimed in the very accents of Papa, but he agreed to let me accompany him.

We drove on for a few hundred yards, until we found a spreading elm with room to hide the carriage beneath it, out of view of a casual observer. From there we proceeded on foot, I clutching my poker, Mullard a stout branch he had picked up from the road. A sign showed the beginning of Abbey Road, where yet another problem faced us. There were two cottages, kitty-cornered.

"Which one would it be? I wonder." Mullard said.

"That one," I said, pointing to a plaster-and-timber cottage. "It has an empty field beyond. Jocko said a balloon ascended from there. It would not have gone up from the middle of a forest."

We studied the cottage for signs of action. There were lights in the front rooms downstairs. The back of the lower story and the whole upper story were in darkness.

"We'll sneak up and take a peek in the windows," I said. "But we must be careful. They might have someone on guard outside."

"One way to find out," Mullard said.

We advanced closer, hiding behind trees, and he threw a stone. It landed with an audible sound at the doorstep. No one came out of the shadows to investigate. He tossed a few more stones, and when he was assured that the house was not guarded from the outside, we crept closer. The curtains were all drawn, making it impossible for us to see what was going forth inside.

"It seems we got here before the others," Mullard said.

"With our late start and slow progress through London, I do not think it at all likely. They must be inside already. Why would it be so silent, unless—" My voice broke on a hiccup of fear.

"Nay, miss. This is no time to put yourself

in a pother. I'll try to get into the house by the back way."

"Let us put our ear to the door first," I said. Now that the actual confrontation was upon us, I found my spirit was willing, but the flesh was weak. The courage required of a cleric's daughter is seldom of the physical sort. The bravest act I had ever performed in my life was to rescue Ginnie Simpson from a dog that was nipping her ankles. I had been ten years old at the time.

"I wonder where they have the lass," Mullard said in a sad voice. "Locked in a room abovestairs, I daresay."

With a thought of Anne's courage and Algernon's danger, I took myself by the scruff of the neck and crept up the two wooden steps to the front door. I was about to place my ear against it when an explosive sound reverberated from within. Not a pistol shot as I first thought, but a heavier, muffled thud, as of a body being hurled to the ground.

In my mind's eye, it was Algernon who was being treated so roughly. Another banging sound followed the first. That one was sharper, perhaps a chair breaking.

"We must go in, Mullard," I said, and put my hand on the doorknob. It did not turn. "It's locked!"

"I'll try the back. You stay here," Mullard said.

I knew he was only trying to protect me, and followed him. The back door was unlocked. I felt certain they would have locked it, and equally sure that Sharkey had had his way with the mechanism, which hung loosely. Once in the house, the sounds of violence increased

181

greatly. A woman was screaming in French. A shot rang out, followed immediately by another. I ran through the kitchen to the parlor and saw Algernon pummeling Vivaldi, while a blowsy blond female screamed and tried to get at Algernon with a water jug. Algernon was in no danger from the older, slimmer Vivaldi. Looking around, I saw where the real danger lay. A man, a dark, handsome man, presumably Alfonse, was pointing a pistol at the fighting men, waiting his chance to shoot without hitting Vivaldi.

When I saw that pistol taking aim at Algernon, all thoughts of fear fell from me. I ran forth like a demon, brandishing my poker. Alfonse spotted me as I went for him. He turned his pistol on me. The others saw me then. Algernon shouted "Cathy!" in a high, incredulous voice. Then a dead silence fell on the room. It was Alfonse's innate sense of decorum that saved my life. For a fraction of a second he hesitated to shoot a lady. It was long enough for me to hit him one good blow on the side of the head with the poker. It did not fell him, but it stunned him for an instant, which allowed Mullard to grab his hands and wrench them behind his back. Alfonse's pistol clattered to the floor. I snatched it up.

"Something to bind this rogue's wrists," Mullard said.

I tore off Alfonse's cravat and held the gun on him while Mullard bound his hands behind his back. Madame went from shrieks to tears. Vivaldi's strength was spent. He rattled off a cannonade of French that sounded like curses, while Algernon pushed him into a chair and tied him up with Madam's lace shawl. They did not bother tying Madam up. She had flung herself at Alfonse, whom she subjected to verbal abuse, alternating with crying and occasionally bestowing moist kisses on his cheeks.

"Where is Anne?" I asked Algernon.

He looked at me in confusion, still not believing his eyes. "How did you get here? What are you doing?"

"Later, Algernon. Where is Anne?"

"Sharkey and Butler went upstairs to look for her. They both went; we had no idea how many might be guarding her. We hoped we could get her out without this crew knowing we were here. I was standing guard in the kitchen to stop them if they overheard and came to stop us. It seems Alfonse was lurking about outside and saw us come in."

"He followed you from London."

"Ah... That explains why you are here. But it does not excuse it! Why the devil—?"

He was interrupted by the sound of thumping feet descending from above. It was Sharkey. He took a look around and said, "I see you don't need my help, folks. There's another one tied up upstairs. I left him on the bed, where they had Annie laid out. Miss Irving, what—?"

"Laid out!" I shouted. "Sharkey, is she—?"

"Drugged. Butler's hauling her down. Here he is now. Can I give you a hand, Butler?"

Butler came down slowly, cradling his beloved Anne in his arms. His left eye was purpling and puffy, but he was smiling softly. "She is breathing. I think she'll be all right," he announced. "We must get her to a doctor at once."

"I'll fetch the carriage," Mullard said, and went out.

We found Butler and Anne a seat on the sofa, and I examined her. Her color was good, and her breathing steady. As she was unconscious, we could not feed her wine. I agreed with Butler that she would be all right in the morning.

"Perhaps now she will have me," he said shyly. "I mean to say, I am not a war hero like her husband, but demme, I would walk through fire for her."

"She will be greatly impressed with this night's work," I told him. Then I left them alone and went to Algernon.

"What will you do with these Frenchmen?" I asked him.

"Jocko mentioned something about bringing a constable. It went against the pluck for him to voluntarily approach the law, but as the team he was driving was not stolen, he agreed to do it. You take Anne home, Cathy. Take her to Papa. She will be looked after properly there."

"No, Algie. She will want to be with Jamie."

"You are right, of course. Home is where the heart is. I shall join you as soon as possible."

"Are you sure you'll be all right?"

Sharkey said, "I told you I'd take care of him for you, Miss Irving. You go home and put on that kettle. Demme, forget the kettle. Bust open a bottle of your aunt's best wine."

"I do not have any wine, Mr. Sharkey."

"She keeps the good stuff in the second room of the cellar, under a pile of wood. I left you a couple of bottles," he said, and laughed.

"So you did steal my wine!"

"Just joshing, Miss Irving. Would I steal from you?"

"Why not? You steal from everyone else."

"Not from friends! And we're good pals."

A reluctant smile stole across my lips. "Then perhaps you will return the wine."

"Too late. It's already sold, but I can buy it back for you at a good price."

Mullard soon arrived with the carriage. Algernon helped settle Anne in on one banquette, with Butler holding her. Before I got in, Algernon said, "It was foolhardy of you to come here, Cathy. Why did you do it?" His voice was tense.

"Why do you think?" I asked, peering at him through the shadows.

"To rescue Anne?"

"That, too."

The expression that seized his handsome features was not a smile, exactly. It was a look of deep satisfaction, tinged with triumph. He took my two hands and held them, then drew me a little away from the carriage door, into the concealing shadows.

"I have tried, but I find I cannot wait to get to Wild Street to tell you how much I love you, Catherine," he said—in a voice made husky with emotion. It flitted through my mind that he, like Miss Thackery, reverted to my formal name at an important moment.

His eyes were two glittering diamonds in the darkness. They drew close, gazing intently at me all the while, as if to absorb my likeness into his mind forever. I closed my eyes as his lips found mine At the first hesitant touch, my heart fluttered like the wings of a thrush, and my lips—my whole body—quivered. He pressed my trembling lips firmly, and the flutter in my heart became a roar, echoing in my ears.

Then he crushed me into his arms, and the roar became a distant echo of heavenly bells, while the kiss deepened to abandonment. After risking life and limb, it seemed natural to risk my heart as well. This was not the time to hold back. His lips demanded a total commitment, and promised the same in return. My thoughts were not so reasoned as I made them sound, but there was a feeling of inevitability and "forever" in that kiss. It was not the practiced performance of the flirt I had first known.

My body felt warm and light, with love swelling inside me like the hot air in a balloon, ready to take off into the blue sky. It was only Algernon's arms, holding me tightly, that kept me tethered to the ground. After a long, leisurely embrace, he slowly released me. He brushed my cheek with his warm fingers. His lightest touch sent another disturbing tremble through me.

He pressed a fleeting kiss on my eyes, my nose, my cheek, like a benediction. "We shall continue this delightful exercise very soon," he said, then we returned to the carriage and were off to Wild Street. Algernon stood, looking after us.

Chapter Eighteen

Miss Thackery was waiting for me at the door with fear in one eye and fire in the other. When she saw me safely home, her anxiety found its customary outlet in verbal abuse.

"What do you mean, Catherine, rushing out of the house in the middle of the night? And

Mullard aiding and abetting you! I shall notify your papa of this."

"We got Anne home safely, so you must not scold," I said, and kissed her roundly on the cheek.

She looked over my shoulder, spotted Butler carrying Anne, and rushed out to meet them. "Is she all right? Oh, my, she looks like death. What have they done to her? And you, Mr. Butler! Your eye is all purple." I had seldom seen Miss Thackery so close to hysterics.

"There was a bit of a scrap, but I am fine," Butler said.

He carried Anne straight upstairs to Miss Lemon. Anne was beginning to show signs of awakening. She was put into bed, and Mullard went off for a doctor. We left Butler upstairs, and I took Miss Thackery back down to give her an expurgated account of my night's doings. I told her that Algernon had discovered, through a friend of Sharkey's, where Anne had been taken, and they went to rescue her. A young woman had come to the door and warned me Alfonse was spying, so I had Mullard go after Algernon to warn him. Yes, there had been a little altercation—during which Butler got hit in the eye—but the constable had come, and all was well now.

"I trust you remained in the carriage, Catherine, and did not go hurling yourself into the midst of spies and guns."

"I was in no danger," I assured her. She took this for confirmation that I had remained in the carriage.

"I hope this running around town like a hurly-burly girl does not give Lord Algernon a disgust of you," was her only remonstrance.

187

Even that was cut short by the arrival of a very dignified-looking gentleman driving a crested carriage and escorted by two liveried postboys. I discerned traces of Algernon in his face and bearing. He was carrying a black bag.

"I am sorry to call at such an hour," he said, "but it is most urgent that I see Mr. Alger."

"Lord Dolman?" I ventured. He gave me a startled look.

"Lord Algernon should be along presently. The…matter has been taken care of satisfactorily."

I could see he did not like to speak, for fear of revealing state secrets. To set him at his ease I said, "We know the whole, my lord. If that black bag contains the five thousand ransom, you may return it to the Horse Guards."

"I see my son has been indiscreet," he said, rather angrily. "As you appear to know things you should not, perhaps you would tell me if he has found Mrs. Clarke."

"She is upstairs in bed. The doctor should be arriving any moment. We do not believe she has been harmed, but she has been drugged."

He nodded in satisfaction. "When you say the matter was taken care of… ?" He looked at Miss Thackery as if he disliked to speak in front of her.

I introduced her. She suggested a cup of tea, and Dolman accepted, to be rid of her. I invited him into the saloon. He sat down, his eyes skimming the room, trying not to reveal their distaste.

I said, "Professor Vivaldi, Alfonse, and Madame Lalonde are being taken into custody. Alger—Lord Algernon—believes Professor Vivaldi is in charge of the spying operation."

I outlined the night's happenings, and Lord Dolman did me the courtesy of listening without interrupting. As I spoke, his stiff demeanor melted to approval.

"By God, you are an extraordinary woman, Miss—What the deuce is your name? You never told me."

"I am Miss Irving—and I am more accustomed to hearing myself called a lady, milord," I said, as he was smiling. I wished to apprise him of that fact, as I felt Algernon would soon be asking his papa's approval to marry me.

"You must forgive me, Miss Irving. The excitement of your news— What the devil is a nice girl like you doing in a hovel like this?"

"I have just recently inherited it from my aunt."

"Ah, you are Thal Cummings's niece. A lovely woman—er, lady. And you plan to continue running the house as your aunt did?"

"Since becoming a little embroiled in the doings of my tenants, I confess I dislike to sell the house out from under them, for it is hard to find a respectable, cheap place to live."

"Just so, and it shows a good profit as well, I should think?"

"Better than Consols," I agreed.

He gave a smile not unlike Colonel Jack's and moved his chair closer. "By Jove, you really are a clever minx. And pretty as well. Still, no reason you must live here to run the house. Hire a housekeeper. I see you in a tidy little cottage in Camden Town, or a flat in the West End..."

He was either thirsty, or forgot about the tea, for he rose and poured two glasses of brandy, handing one to me. When he sat down, he joined me on the sofa. I was beginning to feel uncomfortable, and when his arm slipped around my waist, there was no longer any ignoring his intentions.

I leapt up and said, "Lord Dolman! I must tell you, Lord Algernon—"

"Beat me to it, has he, the sly rogue? I might have known—and he not saying a word to his old papa. Never mind, Miss Irving. You can sit down. I never poach on another fellow's territory, especially my own son's."

It was clear to the meanest intelligence that he took me for a lightskirt. Before I could enlighten him, the doctor and Miss Thackery arrived simultaneously. I was eager to escape, and led the doctor upstairs while Miss Thackery served the tea. I stayed upstairs as long as possible, for I did not know how to treat Lord Dolman. I did not wish to come to cuffs with him, yet I could not allow him to take such freedoms as he had been taking.

Anne had awoken, and her first request was for Jamie. I went into her chamber to find Butler sitting by her bedside, holding her hand and smiling like a moonling. Jamie slept in his crib. All was well. I could not even discover which curl was missing.

"I see there is no need to ask if you are all right, Anne," I said.

She assured me she had not been molested by her abductors. It seemed the promise of a high ransom had kept Alfonse in check. Best of all, she had caught a glimpse of the English traitor through the keyhole at the shop and could identify him. She described a tall gentleman, middle-aged, with a receding hairline.

Butler listened impatiently to this. He had other news to announce. His face told the story without the necessity of words, but before much longer he said, "Anne has agreed to marry me, Miss Irving. We mean to do it up as soon as possible. Money will be tight now that she is out of work, but I shall work my fingers to the bone for her—and Jamie."

It darted into my head that moment that I would ask Anne to be housekeeper for this house. And if Florie returned, I would ask her to help out. Mary was only here temporarily, and Anne would need help—with the baby to look after as well as the house.

I suggested this to them. Anne's look of dazed happiness was answer enough. "And I can stay home with Jamie," she said. "Oh, thank you, Miss Irving."

I left them to their well-earned happiness and returned belowstairs. Miss Thackery appeared to have convinced Lord Dolman we were not the sort of "women" he had taken me for. The talk was all of Radstock, and Papa's parish, and such polite things.

It was well past midnight when Lord Dolman rose. "I have kept you ladies up unpardonably late. It seems Algernon has been delayed. You might tell him I called. I shall expect to see him tomorrow, either at home, or at the Horse Guards. I am very happy to have made your acquaintance, ladies." He bowed and left, with a sheepish glance at me. "Sorry about— Ahem. No hard feelings," he murmured in passing.

"We might as well retire, Cathy," Miss Thackery said. "We can hear all the details from

191

Lord Algernon tomorrow. His papa is very nice, is he not? Not at all high in the instep."

"Yes, very nice," I said... in a choked voice.

Miss Thackery went to bed, but I remained in the saloon longer. I knew I would not sleep until I heard Algernon and Sharkey arrive. My thoughts roamed over the past week and all the unusual occurrences—more happenings than I had experienced in a whole life at Radstock. I had met rogues and scoundrels who stole my belongings; I had met a Bow Street Runner and spies and lords—and it was difficult to say which was worse than the other. I had been propositioned by a drunken colonel and an illustrious member of the House of Lords. I had seen more heroism in a young widow than in the rest of them put together. And best of all, I had found love.

In a benign mood, I concluded that Mrs. Hennessey was not so bad as I had thought. Like everyone else, she was just trying to survive from day to day. It was not easy for her, with two daughters to raise by herself. And it was not easy for Papa, either. A minister needs a wife. Miss Thackery and I had helped with the parish work, but when the work is done, a man wants a special someone to come home to.

I must have fallen into a doze, for I did not hear Algernon come in. When I opened my eyes, he was gazing down at me with such tenderness that it made me feel cherished above diamonds.

"Your papa was here, Algernon," I said, shaking myself awake.

"I have been home. He told me all about it... and apologized," he said, biting back a grin.

Sharkey's crocodile smile appeared around Algernon's elbow. "Can you two lovebirds control yourselves long enough for a little drink to celebrate the occasion? You done good, Miss Irving."

"Thank you, Sharkey, but—"

He held out a dusty bottle of wine, presumably retrieved from beneath the woodpile. He poured three glasses and proposed a toast. "To me," he said. "Eric P. Sharkey. This is the first time I ever put myself in danger for anything but money. I'm a hero, that's what I am—or a fool." He tilted his glass and emptied it.

"You are a hero, Sharkey. You did it for England," I said.

"I'll expect a reward," he said, looking hopefully to Algernon. "What has England ever done for me? Was Bow Street here?" was his next question. No tremble of fear shot through me.

"No. What have you prigged, Sharkey?"

"Prigged? I ain't a thief. I'm a wholesaler of odd lots. Ned was supposed to drop off the muslin and silk he napped from Lalonde. I have a customer in Cheapside I promised it to."

"Don't bring it into this house."

"I told him to leave it at the back door. There is a bolt of blue shot silk there, Miss Irving. It would make a dandy wedding outfit." He gave a lecherous little "Heh-heh," and stared at us, as if expecting Algernon to fall to his knees and propose.

"Why do you not give the silk to Anne?" I suggested. "She and Butler were smelling of April and May when she woke up. They are going to marry very soon."

"High time he made an honest woman of her."

"You are incorrigible!" I scolded, and blushed to recall I had accused her of being Algernon's mistress.

Sharkey said, "I'll sell the silk to Butler." I gave a *tsk*. "At a good price! He'd pay twice as much in a shop."

Algernon smiled tolerantly. "Why do you not ask him now?" he suggested, to be rid of Sharkey.

"A good idea. If I make the sale in front of Mrs. Clarke, he'll be ashamed to haggle."

He left, and I told Algernon that Anne had caught a glimpse of the English traitor and was willing to identify him. From the description, Algernon felt sure it was Makepiece.

We sat side by side on the sofa. He took my hand and squeezed it. "Papa tells me you are thinking of keeping the house, Cathy."

"Yes, but I shan't go on living here myself."

"You will be happier at Grosvenor Square," he said, peering for my reaction. "That is an offer of marriage, my dear." I just sat, dazed with happiness. "Is that a yes?"

"Oh, yes! Yes, indeed."

We celebrated the betrothal with a kiss, and then another. Before we were properly finished, I drew back and said "Grosvenor Square? I thought you lived on Berkeley Square?"

"I did, but as it seems Papa has also become enamored of you..."

"He thought I was a lightskirt, Algie!"

"I rang a loud peal over him, I promise you. It would have been louder—had I not made the same mistake myself when we first met."

"Like father, like son."

"It is the fact of your living in this house. As

194

you can have few illusions after this adventure, I might as well tell you the whole. Your aunt was Papa's... er..."

"Mistress!" Once the first shock was over, I realized I had suspected Thalassa of being no better than she should for some time. Those garish gowns, the very fact of her living in this neighborhood... The greatest surprise was that she had a noble patron.

"Just so. That is why Papa chose this house for Anne when she came to us. She had been living in rooms at the edge of Long Acre. She could have afforded a little better, I think, but she was determined to save enough money to educate Jamie. She would not accept payment for her services. Remarkable, is it not? I occasionally prevailed on her to take a few trifles she required." I thought of the chiffonier, and the watch.

"Your aunt kept an eye on her, and of course I did likewise, with Miss Lemon's and Sharkey's help," Algernon continued. "Your aunt's death just as the affair reached its climax was a severe blow. Then you came, insisting you would sell the place. Not that one can blame you, of course. This is no place for a lady, mixing with such rogues as Sharkey."

"No, I will not have you disparage my house, or my tenants! I have decided they are all nature's ladies and gentlemen. I want them to stay, but when I find a replacement for Vivaldi, I shall be a little more choosy."

"You will require a permanent housekeeper."

"I already have one. Anne has agreed to do it. She will do an excellent job, and she will be happier at home with Jamie than going out to

195

work. It will ease the financial strain for them as well, if they do not have to pay rent."

"An excellent idea! Papa was right. You really are an extraordinary woman. Er... lady."

"The sooner we are married, the better. When I am Lady Algernon, this doubt as to my gentility will disappear."

"I could not agree with you more. In the meanwhile, let us enjoy Miss Irving."

His embrace was not all gentlemanly, but Miss Irving enjoyed it very much.

If you have enjoyed reading this large print book and you would like more information on how to order a Wheeler Large Print book, please write to:

 Wheeler Publishing, Inc.
P.O. Box 531
Accord, MA 02018-0531

R&